MAGGIE'S MISTAKE

MAGGIE'S MISTAKE

•

Carolyn Brown

AVALON BOOKS
NEW YORK

Library of Congress Catalog Card Number: 2002093585
ISBN 0-8034-9576-5

Published by Thomas Bouregy & Co., Inc.
160 Madison Avenue, New York, NY 10016

PRINTED IN THE UNITED STATES OF AMERICA
ON ACID-FREE PAPER
BY HADDON CRAFTSMEN, BLOOMSBURG, PENNSYLVANIA

With much love to
Mildred Edwards
who will always be my
favorite aunt!

Chapter One

Everett Dulanis was dreaming of his sweet Carolina's pretty blue eyes when something cold awoke him with a start. The chilly barrels of a shotgun were pressed right between his brown eyes, which suddenly popped open wide as he tried to figure out in his half-asleep, half-awake state just why someone would want to kill him. He must still be dreaming, because he was on a straw tick mattress in a dugout house with a strange red-haired woman wrapped in nothing but a thin blanket snuggled against his side, but it sure seemed real enough. It had to be the most vivid dream he'd ever had in his entire life—he could feel the chill of the gun barrels on his skin and his life had begun to flash before him.

"I reckon it's time you wake up and get ready to pay the price for your wicked night or else take both these shells in your head, Doc," the man holding the gun said.

Everett was not dreaming.

Four other men crowded down the steps and stopped in their tracks when they saw the sight before them. The new doctor in Dodsworth, Indian Territory and Maggie Listen wrapped up together in a couple of worn-out blankets. By the bareness of her shoulders and legs, there wasn't much left to the imagination about what went on in that old abandoned dugout house.

"Get on out of here. Ain't a one of you got any business lookin' on my daughter like that." Ben Listen shooed them away with his gun, then pointed it right back at Everett's head.

From his viewpoint, each one of those barrels looked big enough to drive a team and freight wagon into. He didn't know whether to start explaining the whole story before or after he got his clothes back on. Now that he was fully awake he realized what was going on. Appearances were certainly deceiving. If Ben would just put down the blunderbuss and listen to reasoning, he'd understand. Somehow the look in the older man's angry blue eyes told Everett no matter how fast and furious he explained, there was still going to be a bloodletting.

"Mmmm," Maggie moaned lightly in her sleep and threw an arm over Everett's chest. Ben didn't need any more proof. He had his gun. It was Sunday morning. He knew where the preacher was, and this hoity-toity doctor from back east had just better stand right up there and promise to love, honor, and respect Maggie until death do them part . . . or else he could have the death part right then and there.

"Maggie," Everett said lightly without taking his eyes from the gun barrels which were looking bigger with each passing moment.

"Good grief!" She sat straight up and opened her green eyes wide. "Daddy, what are you doing here? Put that stupid gun down. For goodness sake, you might hurt someone with that blunderbuss. I can explain all this. It's sure not what it looks like right now," she said, drawing the thin blanket closer to her naked chest.

"Ain't no explainin' to do or undo. I ain't blind, Maggie. You turn your face over and look out that window and don't you turn back around until the doctor here gets all his clothing back on. Then him and me will go outside with the boys and we'll wait for you to come out fully dressed. Then we're going right to the church and the preacher is going to marry you two up. I ain't havin' talk and there ain't no explainin' this," Ben said flatly.

"But, Mr. Listen, we didn't." Everett used the blanket as a shield as he put first one leg and then another into his long union suit, still not completely dry. "I mean, it's really not like it looks. We got soaked and the buggy overturned and the horse ran away."

"I'm not interested in listenin' to you, Doc. Finish gettin' dressed and don't try to run or nothin'. Never thought I'd see the day I took my shotgun to the wedding for Maggie, but I'm not havin' people talk about her. So you'll marry her or die." Ben popped the gun back up on his shoulder.

"I'm not marryin' nobody." Maggie raised her voice and started to turn around.

"Don't you dare look around here." Ben's voice would have put icicles on Saint Lucifer's pitchfork. "The man ain't dressed and even if you two was wicked last night, you won't be again until you're proper married up."

"Well, I'm not marrying Dr. Everett. You can just shoot him and me both and get it over with. I'm not marryin' no man who can't laugh and who can't dance and I durn sure ain't marryin' a man I don't love," she declared with a defiant flip of her deep red hair.

"You better get control of that tongue of yours, Maggie. Your Momma would wash your mouth out with lye soap for using them kind of words. If you ain't going to marry him, then I'll just blow his brains out right here and take you home to live in shame the rest of your natural days," Ben said. "Might have to shoot lots of men before you die. They'll all come sniffin' around our back door like hound dogs when they find out how easy you was. We're goin' outside now. I expect you to have your clothes on in five minutes, girl, and come out that door without a bit of sass. You should have thought of the fact he couldn't dance and he don't make you laugh before you bedded down with him last night."

"I didn't bed down with him," Maggie said. "We was

soaked to the skin so we took off our clothes to dry and wrapped up in them two blankets. If you had a brain, Daddy, you'd see that we was both wrapped up separate. Not together."

"Don't matter now how you was wrapped up. You're going to get hitched up with him and I'll not hear another word," Ben said, nodding toward the fully clad doctor to proceed before him up the steps and into the crisp fall Sunday morning.

"I want you all to know that nothing happened here last night," Everett said to the men staring at him outside the dugout. "Maggie got left at the dance and I volunteered to bring her back to Dodsworth. The storm got worse and worse. Lightning hit a big tree and spooked my horse. He went wild and the buggy overturned. You can find it back down the road a ways. The horse broke the reins and ran away and it was pouring down rain. Maggie happened to remember this old dugout house and we ran all the way here. We were soaked but there was a couple of dry blankets in the place. So we each turned our backs and undressed, wrapped up in the blankets and waited out the storm. I guess we fell asleep," Everett said.

I can't dance and I can't laugh. Suddenly the words stung his ego. *Good grief, who does she think she is to say anything about me. She might be able to dance and goodness knows she can laugh. But she's about as intelligent as a box of rocks.*

"And that's the way it is, and I'm not marrying Doc. I don't love him and he don't love me. I won't marry up with no man when there's no love," Maggie said matter-of-factly as she stepped out of the dugout to the bright sunshine of a beautiful fall day.

"All the talk in the world don't undo what the eyes have seen," Ben said. "Now you two get in the wagon. There's room for all of us on the seat. Reckon it won't hurt none for you to sit beside her real close in view of the fact we're on the way to the church. It ain't the kind of wedding I'd planned to give you. Always figured it that you'd wear your Momma's white dress like your older sister did and stand up in the church house and have a big party afterwards. But you done made your choice and that is the way it'll be."

Everett was glad he had a very good lawyer friend in the state of Georgia. If Ben didn't come to his senses on the way to Dodsworth and really did make him marry the sassy red-haired baggage, then he'd simply telegraph James and tell him to prepare an annulment. Lord, but Carolina was going to have a fit. But maybe, just maybe, things could be done so quietly Carolina wouldn't have to know about it. He'd give Maggie enough money to send her far away with the instructions that there would be more if she never showed her face in Dodsworth again.

Yeah, right. By noon, little bitty town like Dodsworth is going to be buzzing with the news that you married the girl. You think Carolina is going to come here to live and not find out the first five minutes after she gets into town that you married another woman and why?

Everett shook his head. Carolina was a grown woman, and she'd simply understand when he explained the whole thing to her. She wasn't a country bumpkin in a green cotton dress with a one-track mind on dancing. She was a cultured southern woman who was as intelligent as she was beautiful. She'd simply brush the whole affair off as what it was. A silly mistake. They might even laugh about the whole thing after he went to Georgia for the wedding and brought her home to Dodsworth to live happily ever after.

"Daddy, you have got to listen to me," Maggie said in exasperation. "Think back. You brought two wagons of us to the dance. I was in the other wagon when it was time to go home but I forgot my hat. Left it laying on a table in the barn. One of them ornery Johnson boys had thrown it up to the hay mow and it was stuck on a nail. Took me a good ten minutes to get it off, but I did. Then when I got outside there wasn't a soul there except the doctor here, and he was already driving away. We started out and it commenced to lightning. Can't you believe me?"

"I believe everything you and the Doc said. Every word of it. I also believe what I saw in that room. Don't matter to me if not one thing happened. What it looked like is what I do mind, Maggie Listen. Nobody in Logan County would believe you two slept together wound up like a couple of newborn baby piglets and nothing happened. So you're marryin' this man soon as we get to the church."

"That is crazy," Maggie snapped.

"Might be, but that's the way it's going to be." Ben nodded and slapped the reins to make the horses go a little faster. The sooner this thing was done the better.

The sun rose in a bright orange ball in the east. Dew sparkled like diamonds. Leaves still hung onto the tree limbs but were an artist's palette in a wild array of oranges, crimsons, and lemon yellow. Everything kept right on doing what it knew to do. The sun was rising in spite of the fact Maggie's heart was a ball of stone laying in her chest. The seasons were changing just like they always did. But who would have guessed yesterday morning that today she'd be on the way to her wedding. Not in a flowing white dress that Violet sewed for her, or even her Momma's dress that waited in the rolltop trunk in the attic. Not with Emma and Jed standing up with her and her groom, but with a shotgun for a maid of honor and best man rolled into one. Did her daddy plan to blow a hole in the marriage license instead of having witnesses sign it?

Fall was Everett's favorite season. A time when the heat of summer faded and before the cold bitter winds of winter were born. A time when the harvest was reaped and the earth rested from her labors for a few months. He'd chosen fall for his wedding to Carolina on purpose for that reason. He saw himself waiting on the stairs of the mansion at her father's huge plantation and letting his heart lift up to hers as she descended, her golden hair the brilliant color of the morning sun, the diamond on her left hand sparkling like the dew on the ground.

His dream had just turned into his worst nightmare. Maggie's dress was just as damp as his own black suit. A smudge of dirt streaked across her neck, and hay was strewn in her almost crimson red hair. Her mossy green eyes were circled with dark rings, proving that she hadn't slept any better than he had, and there were little specks of sleep still clinging to the inside corners of her eyes. All this trouble because he had been a true southern gentleman and offered to take her home. Five minutes. Just five more minutes and he would have been on down the road, and she could have spent the night in the barn where the dance had been held. When Ben came hunting for her he would have found her sleeping in the barn . . . alone.

Maggie wanted to shove both the men out in the road, grab the reins, and drive the horses all the way to Texas. If she'd been smart enough to pack her gun in her reticule, she'd have held her own father off at gunpoint and let Everett escape while her dad came to his senses. Lord, just the thought of being married to Dr. Everett Dulanis gave her a case of the hives. Granted he was good-looking in a dark, brooding way. Lots of the girls in Logan County had whispered about how they'd like to be the one he was engaged to—but not Maggie. She didn't like those dark brooding eyes or that wavy black hair. All of it made a man who was entirely too serious for her dream husband.

"Daddy, you are forgetting something," she said, grasping at elusive straws. "Dr. Everett is engaged. Remember, he's going to Georgia in a couple of weeks to get married."

"Hmphh." Ben snorted. "He should have thought about that before now. He's getting married today in Dodsworth. Whatever he was going to do in Georgia is over with."

Maggie sighed. Dr. Everett was going to hate her for sure. He'd never even looked at one of the local ladies. The only time she ever knew him to even have a bit of conversation with them was when they were needing his doctoring services or else for a formal dance around the barn, and then it was just being nice. He loved his southern lady with all his heart, but in an hour he was going to be dead or married to Maggie Listen. He'd rather be dead, she was sure. She smoothed out the front of her green dress and fought back a river of tears. Neither of the pompous men she rode with would see her cry, not if she had to bite blood from the inside of her lip. It was a shame that women had no more rights than they did. It flat out wasn't fair. She didn't want to be married to Everett Jackson Dulanis, and there wasn't a single reason why she should have to marry him. Except that women had to keep a good name and hers had just gone up in flames on a straw tick in an abandoned dugout house.

Everett held his chin high. He was through explaining and trying to reason with Ben Listen. No wonder Maggie was mentally deficient. She inherited the trait from her obstinate father. He'd have to marry the girl. No doubt the legalities would then take long enough that he and Carolina would have to postpone their wedding until after the new year. But he'd do it like the gentleman he was raised to be and not like a sniveling coward. It didn't matter that his suit was wrinkled and looked like he'd slept in it, or that his trousers were splattered with dried mud. It wasn't a real marriage and they wouldn't be real vows he spoke before the preacher in the church house. It was nothing short of a farce; the vows he said wouldn't be anything but shotgun vows.

"Okay," Ben said after an hour of heavy silence. "Here we are. Don't try nothing funny now, Doc. I'd just as soon shoot you as look at you right now. And there ain't a jury in Logan County would string me up for it, neither."

Everett gave him his most piercing, stoic stare and simply walked into the church ahead of the other two. He didn't wait to hold the door for Maggie or to explain anything to Preacher Elgin, who was busy laying hymnals on the pews. He'd marry the girl, but there would never be a marriage. Not in the real sense of the word. Next week, James would have the papers ready for the annulment.

"Mornin' Doc. What brings you in here so early?" Preacher Elgin asked.

"He's here to marry up with Maggie," Ben said from the doorway. His shotgun rested easily under his arm. "They spent the night together up in that old dugout. So he's here to make an honest woman out of my little girl."

Preacher Elgin raised an eyebrow at Everett. "That true?"

"No, it's not," Maggie said, her whole face skewed up in a frown. "I mean we spent the night together and we took off our clothes because they got wet in the storm but that's all that happened, Preacher Elgin. We didn't do one thing. He didn't even kiss me goodnight."

"You got some of them marriage licenses?" Ben asked. "I want this done up right."

"Well," Preacher Elgin wanted to lie so bad his heart ached from it, but he couldn't force the word no from his mouth. If he hadn't picked up a couple of licenses at the Logan County Courthouse last week, these two kids might have had a chance. By morning, someone might be able to talk sense to Ben. But then, probably not. Ben Listen was as stubborn headed as any cross-eyed mule the preacher had ever seen.

"You got one or not? I can drive them over to Guthrie and wake up the Justice of the Peace. I'm sure he's got one of them licenses." Ben waved the gun at the preacher.

"Yes, I have some right here." Preacher Elgin pulled a long piece of paper from the shelf under the pulpit. "But you'll have to take it to the courthouse tomorrow morning and get it registered or it ain't legal."

"I'll be sittin' on their doorstep when they open the doors. You just fill it in and say the right words to make it legal. I'll do the rest," Ben said seriously.

"All right," Preacher Elgin said, his heart lying in his chest almost as heavy as he figured Maggie's and Everett's were. "But wait a minute. Dr. Everett is engaged. Ben, we can't do this."

"We can and we will. He should have thought of that before he ruined my daughter's name. Them all wrapped up in blankets on a straw tick and four other men seeing them that way. His engagement is over. Now get your ink out, preacher, and fix that paper," Ben said.

"Maggie, what is your middle name?" The preacher opened the bottle of ink and picked up a pen.

"Laura," she said.

"And yours?" He turned to the doctor.

"Jackson," he said without a bit of warmth in his voice.

"Who are we going to get to witness this marriage?" Preacher Elgin asked.

"I'll be one and . . ." Ben looked around the empty church. "She can be the other one," he said when Preacher Elgin's wife came in the back door.

"Okay, then, we will begin. Doc, you stand right here. Maggie, you stand beside him," Preacher Elgin said.

"What is going on here?" Myrtle Elgin demanded.

"My daughter is being made an honest woman out of and you're going to witness," Ben said.

"I'm not witnessing anything until I know what has happened," Myrtle declared.

"I'm tired of all this talk," Ben said, his eyes flashing anger. "This shotgun says there's going to be a wedding. You're going to witness or I'm going to shoot this philandering fool right between his eyes. So stand up here and when it's done you can sign your name that you saw the preacher marry them."

"Then just shoot him," Myrtle said. "I'm not witnessing a marriage between two people who look like they'd rather be dead as married. A marriage is supposed to have some love in it. This one ain't got a bit."

"Amen," Maggie said. "But I reckon you'd do well to go ahead and do what he says. He's got his heart set on the doctor making me his wife. And I don't think he's going to listen to any kind of sense, not with that gun. He hasn't in the last hour anyway. And I figure he would shoot the doctor in the blink of a frog's eye."

"No," Myrtle said. "You can come and live with us until we figure this out. All our girls are married. We'll take you in."

"You want to be dead with him?" Ben shoved the gun into her face.

"All right. That is enough," Preacher Elgin said. "Dearly beloved, we are gathered here today in the sight of God Almighty and these two witnesses to join Everett Jackson Dulanis and Maggie Laura Listen in holy matrimony . . ."

Never in her life had Maggie wanted so badly to fall down and cry like a baby. Surely this was a dream and she would wake up in a minute in the loft of their cabin with the three single beds lined up in a row. Elenor would be asleep on one side of her and Grace curled up in a ball on the other side.

"Do you, Maggie Laura Listen, take this man to be your lawfully wedded husband? Do you vow to love, honor, and obey him through sickness and health, through joy and sorrow, good times and bad, until death parts you?"

She just stared at the preacher. How could she make that promise? Ben Listen narrowed his eyes. "I do," she whispered.

"Do you, Everett Jackson Dulanis, take this woman to be your lawfully wedded wife? Do you vow to love, honor, and protect her through sickness and health, through joy and sorrow, good times and bad, until death parts you?"

"I do," he said, hoping that Carolina did understand these backwoods people and their backward ways.

"Then by the authority vested in me by God and by Oklahoma, Indian Territory, I pronounce you man and wife. What God has joined together let no man put asunder. Everett, you may kiss your bride."

"No thank you," Everett said.

"Oh, yes, you will." Ben raised the gun to his shoulder.

"I ain't havin' you slight my girl. You didn't mind sleeping with her last night so you can kiss your bride now. Then you can take her on home."

Everett bent down and brushed a dry kiss across Maggie's mouth. Neither of them closed their eyes. Sparks didn't fly around the room. "How am I supposed to take her home? My buggy is overturned across Bear Creek. My horse ran away," he said.

"Walk. God give you two legs and it's only a little over a mile out to that cabin Emma and Jed is lettin' you live in. Be good for both of you to walk. Don't expect you'll be back in time for church this morning. Maybe that's best. Now put your name on that paper, Myrtle, so I can put mine on it. I'll send Elenor over to your new house with your things this evening, Maggie. I don't reckon you'd better come home to see your Ma for a couple of weeks. You know what a temper that woman has got. By then she'll be over her fit and things might be settlin' down."

"It'll take me way longer than two weeks to want to see you," Maggie said.

"You'll get over it," Ben said, signing the document. He carefully folded it twice and put it in his pocket. "I'll get this to the courthouse tomorrow. You made your bed last night, Maggie. Now you can sleep in it."

"Let's go," Everett said. "We'll sort this all out tomorrow."

"You're right about that." Maggie stomped off ahead of him.

"Good luck," Myrtle said, sympathetically.

We'll need more than luck, Maggie thought as Everett reached her side and they walked out of the church together, anger pouring out of both of them. A union had just taken place, but there wasn't one bit of respect, honor, or love involved in it.

Chapter Two

"Where are you going?" Everett broke the silence when Maggie left Main Street and started off across the rolling hills.

"I'm not walking down Main Street looking like this. Folks will be coming out to go to church. I'm not walking down the road to your cabin, either. I know a shortcut across the land. It won't matter if I get my skirt tails dirty since they're already caked with mud. You can go with me, go back to church, go to your office and stay all day, or go straight to the devil, Everett Dulanis. I'm tired. I didn't go to sleep until daylight and then you know the rest. I'm hungry and I want a bath." With every word, Maggie stomped the wet earth harder and walked faster.

Everett was a tall man and had a long stride but by the time they reached the cabin where he'd been living the past few months, he was winded. Maggie might not be able to carry on a conversation about the problems in the world, but she could sure enough make her way through the trees and underbrush to the back door of his humble home. She didn't wait for him to open the door for her, probably knowing that if he hadn't treated her like a lady up until then, there wasn't any reason to expect him to start now.

"I'm cooking breakfast and then I'm taking the tub into

the bedroom and having a bath. Until I get my stomach full and these damp clothes off my body, I don't intend to discuss any of this mess with you. And that's a fact," she said, going straight for the stove to stoke up a fire.

Everett pulled the tub off the nail beside the back door and drug it into the bedroom. He checked the reservoir on the stove. The water was still fairly warm so he began filling a galvanized milk bucket with warm water and toting it to the tub while Maggie fussed around finding groceries to make breakfast. There wasn't going to be a discussion anyway. He'd have the whole thing undone as quick as telegram service could get it done. James would howl in laughter at the story, but he'd get right on it.

"I'm going to take a bath while you're cooking," he announced, closing the door to his bedroom. He shucked out of his clothing and eased his tired body down into the warm water, shutting his eyes and seeing Carolina's pretty blue twinkling eyes. Surely she would understand this mess he had gotten himself into.

Maggie found flour and soda on the shelf above the work table. The lard and butter would be in the spring house, along with the buttermilk. She'd check for meat while she was there, too. There hadn't been a freeze yet, so bacon and ham would have to wait a month or more, but there could be a hunk of venison or something she could fry up to go along with the eggs she'd found still in a basket beside the pump in the kitchen. Sure enough, there was a slab of pork chops in the spring house. Not sugar cured but still fresh. Jed must have butchered a hog in the last couple of days. Didn't look like a very big one. He'd probably chosen the smallest one just to tide them over until frost, when they could really have a butchering day.

Everett finished bathing, wishing he could wash away the past twenty-four hours like he did the mud and grit from his body. In a bigger place, this ordeal might have ruined his practice. Out here in Indian Territory, it wouldn't really matter who he was married to. Folks could either come to him for his services or go all the way to Guthrie like they'd done until he moved to Dodsworth. They wouldn't care if he'd married Ben Listen's prize hog, long as he could sew them up when the hatchet missed the mark, or set their broken arms. Deliver their babies. Give them medicine for their aches and pains.

The aroma of frying pork chops and onions crept through the crack under the door and his stomach grumbled. Other than a piece of someone's horrid apple pie at the dance the night before, he hadn't eaten since lunch the day before. Twenty four hours . . . again he wished he could go back to lunch that day and start all over.

"It's about ready," Maggie said when he came out of the bedroom. His coal black hair was darker than a raven's tail feather at midnight with droplets of water still hanging onto it. He'd changed into a snowy white shirt and clean dark trousers with a perfect crease up the front. Maggie wondered if perhaps Emma had been doing his laundry.

"Is that onions?" he asked.

"I scattered a few in the fried potatoes. Just got to make the gravy. Why don't you dump that water and when we finish eating, I can get a bath," she said.

"I'll do it after we eat," he said. He'd taken all the orders and suggestions he could stand for one day.

Maggie whipped around to look at him. She'd let him take his bath first. She'd cooked a big breakfast when she wanted to fall in a heap. "Have it your way," she snapped coolly. "Now what are we going to do about this?"

"I thought you were going to eat and take a bath first," he said just as coolly.

"I just changed my mind," she said.

"Well, how did you know where to find all this stuff to cook with?" he asked, changing the subject.

"I was here when Emma and Jed lived here, and I helped Emma lots of times. I was also here when Violet and Orrin lived here. She was in a fire and burned her feet really bad and I came and helped out. I know where everything is in this house. Probably better than you do," she said. "Now, set up to the table and tell me just what we're going to do about this whole mess while we eat."

With the grace of a woman accustomed to cooking, she poured gravy into a bowl and picked up a plate of steaming hot biscuits from the warmer at the top of the stove. She set them on the table and went back for a bowl of light, fluffy scrambled eggs, and then, using the tail of an apron she'd found hanging on a hook just inside the back door, she lifted the iron skillet of fried potatoes and onions and brought it to the table.

"They'll stay hotter in the skillet and not get a grease skim," she said as she put them on a hot pad in the middle of the table. "Now bow your head. We can't thank the Lord for this miserable day but we can thank him for the food."

Everett had never put lighter, fluffier biscuits in his mouth. The gravy was perfect. Not too runny. No lumps. The eggs were straight from Heaven, and the touch of onions in the potatoes complimented the pork chops perfectly. He wondered if, when the whole ordeal of today was sorted through, Maggie might be interested in permanent employment in the house he had designed for Carolina. He'd redesign a room for her just off the kitchen if she'd be willing to hire on as their permanent cook. Carolina couldn't boil water without burning down a plantation. She'd grown up in a wealthy home with cooks, maids, and her own personal servant to wait upon her hand and foot.

Everett had known from the beginning that life wouldn't be easy for his princess Carolina in the territory; but she'd only have to live in the little cabin a few months. Maybe he could talk Maggie into coming in through the days and doing the work and cooking for Carolina. He sipped his coffee. A man's coffee. So strong he couldn't begin to see the bottom of the cup.

"Okay, we've eaten. Now have you got any ideas?" From the far end of the table, Maggie looked at him, expecting answers, although she didn't know why. He had not been able to keep them out of the marriage. Why did she think he could fix it when it was over? Just because he was a doctor didn't give him magical powers.

"My lawyer in Georgia will file annulment papers. I'll have to go to Guthrie tomorrow and send him a telegram, outlining what I need done. Then he'll draw up whatever papers are needed and either send or bring them here. We'll both sign them and that will be it. Do you have a place to go until it's over?" he asked, wishing she wouldn't have any friends who would take her in. He'd give up his bedroom and climb up to the loft every night to have breakfast like this every morning. Emma usually sent down a plate of leftovers when he was too late to eat at her supper table, but he'd been making his own breakfast.

"I could stay with Emma or Violet either one," she said. "But we are married by the law so I could just stay here. You'll be gone all day anyway. Elenor is bringing my stuff later. You sure that lawyer can undo this?"

"Yes, I'm sure, Maggie. And I'd be glad to have you stay here. You can have the bedroom in there." He nodded toward the door. "I'll move my things to the loft."

"Okay," she said. She would have gladly taken the loft. To have the whole thing to herself would have been luxury deluxe after sharing their small loft with her two sisters the past couple of years. But she wasn't going to suggest it. Her own room with a door and a window that looked out at the stars and moon would be the price she charged for cooking his breakfast and doing his laundry until the annulment came through.

"You ever think about working for other folks? When Carolina and I are wed I'd be willing to hire you to cook and clean for us," he said.

A twitch began at the corners of Maggie's full, sensuous mouth and her green eyes sparkled. The first sound from her lips was a ladylike giggle; the next, a very unladylike laugh; the last, a full fledged roar like a miner with cabin fever at the first spring thaw. She wiped her eyes on her apron and got the hiccups. She slapped the table and tried holding her breath, only to break out in another round of giggles.

"What is so funny?" he asked. His dark eyebrows drew together in a single line across his forehead. His mouth pursed so tightly he could scarcely get the words out.

"You." Maggie shook her head. "You had to have a brain to get all that schooling to be a doctor man. You got money 'cause you been saying you're going to build a house for your intended. And you're just living here in this forsaken part of the world because you feel like you can help the folks, according to what Emma told me when I asked what a rich doctor was doing here. But when it comes to common sense, Everett Dulanis, you come up with the short end of the stick."

"And that's so funny you can't breathe?" he asked tersely.

"Your darlin' Carolina is going to scalp you, honey. If she marries you when this is over, it'll be a pure miracle from Heaven. Just coming out to this wilderness from the big city was asking a lot from some southern belle who was raised up rich. But to expect her to have your ex-wife in her house every day is crazy as a loon. She won't want me within a hundred miles of you. After all, she'll never be sure what really did go on in that dugout house or what went on in this house while we waited on them papers, now will she? So Everett, my answer is no. I will not work for you, at least after the papers get here. Until then we are married. On paper anyway."

"Carolina is not that kind of woman. She's a sensitive, kind woman who will understand this situation. She would be glad for you to work for her," he argued.

"Honey, Carolina is a woman. If the thing were reversed, and I was that sensitive kind woman, you'd be out on your ear, and that's a fact. Now I'm going to clean up these dishes while you take that cold water out. Then I'm going to take a bath. I don't suppose you got any clean clothes for a woman hiding in this house?" she asked flatly.

"No, I surely do not!" he exclaimed.

She'd just shown how mentally deficient she really was when she made those comments about his darling fiancée. She didn't know anything about his Carolina. He'd just have to tell Carolina about Maggie and her abilities in the kitchen. When Carolina asked her to work for them, then Maggie would understand just what a lady she really was. He dumped the water on the ground just off the back porch and dragged the tub back to the bedroom. While she washed dishes and put them away, he refilled the tub for her. Even after her smart aleck attitude, he would be a gentleman. She simply didn't understand the ways of the south and probably never would.

"Thank you," she said simply. "Now where are some of your working clothes? Not your good things you wear to the office every day, but a pair of working trousers and a shirt. I'll be hanged from that scrub oak tree out there in the yard before I put these stiff, muddy clothes back on."

"You would wear men's pants?" he asked incredulously. Was there no decency in the woman?

"I'd wear that blanket out of the dugout right now," she said, eyeing him carefully. "I expect your britches will be a little too long and a mite big around the waist since I've got the smallest waist for my height in all Logan County. But I can use a piece of bailing twine to keep them up. I'll wash out my things and hang them on the line. It won't be long until they're dry and I can put them back on. Or else until Elenor comes with my stuff."

He opened the doors to a wardrobe and took out a pair of khaki-colored britches and a blue shirt. Both were unironed and soft. She nodded her thanks and shut the door behind him when he left the room. She dropped her dress, then her camisole and drawers on the floor, along with her petticoats and stockings. The mirror at the top of the chest of drawers showed the dark circles under her eyes and the smear of dirt still on her neck.

"What a lovely bride," she said, a core of sadness radiating sorrow through her entire soul. "Even if I do find a real husband someday, I can never have a real wedding. Divorced. I'll be a marked woman. Will Daddy like that better than a loose woman? Either way, his daughter isn't going to be worth much ever again."

The warmth of the bath water didn't do a thing to ease her depression, which was fast turning into anger. How dare Ben Listen make her marry Everett? It was all his fault anyway. If he'd made sure she was in one of the wagons when they went home, he would have known to wait for her. But no, he just took everyone's word that she was in the other wagon. Just because there was a storm brewing everyone wanted to get home in a hurry. The same storm had sent her and Everett dashing for the first shelter they could find. There just happened to be two blankets in the place. She wouldn't be surprised if her father hadn't left them there himself and planned the whole mess, just so she'd be married. The whole family knew Elenor was pining after Ivan Svenson over on the next farm and Momma said there wasn't no way Elenor was getting married until Maggie did. That was the proper way of things. The oldest daughter first, and then the next one.

Maggie slid down in the tub and ducked her entire head under the water. She wiped her eyes when she surfaced and picked up the bar of soap on the chair beside the tub. The water was soft and she lathered her deep red hair into a crown of rich white soap. She rinsed it out and sat in the bubbles for a long time, trying to figure out just what she would do with her life now that it was ruined. Maybe she'd just ask Everett for enough money to go to California. She might just start up her own little restaurant, making real food and selling it for a good price. It didn't take a full-fledged genius to see the joy in Everett's face when he broke open one of her biscuits and popped it into his mouth.

When the water was too cold to sit in it any longer, she rose up out of it and grabbed the towels Everett had lain on the chair with the soap. She wrapped one around her hair and dried her body with the other one. The shirt was soft but didn't do one thing to harness in her more than ample bosom. She was glad it was a couple of sizes too big, since that covered up the fact she wasn't wearing undergarments. Like she'd said, the pants were several inches too long and too big around her waspy waist. She laced the sash from her green dress through the loops and roped the britches in to fit her.

"Too bad I wasn't born a man," she said, looking in the mirror again. "These britches and simple shirt are sure more comfortable than dresses, corsets, and drawers."

Everett wasn't prepared for what he saw when she threw open the bedroom door and waltzed out. Maggie was built—really built. Her cheeks were rosy from scrubbing and her wet hair fell in a brilliant cascade to her waist. "I'll take care of that water. I hear a wagon coming down the road. It's either Emma and Jed coming home or it's your sister."

"Oh fiddle," she sighed. Either one would see her in britches and that would be all over Dodsworth, too. That she'd made the doctor marry her and then went home to put on his britches.

She'd hardly gotten the thought out when Mary burst through the front door. "Maggie, are you here? You'll never guess what Grace told us at church. She said you and Everett got married this morning oh my goodness what are you doing wearing a man's trousers and on Sunday Preacher Elgin would just curl up and die or else pray for you all day." She rattled on without stopping until her breath gave out.

"Elenor hasn't gotten here yet with my things," Maggie said.

"I understand there's been a problem." Emma swept in behind Mary, and the other kids followed right behind her. Jed carried in the baby, Lalie Joy, as he brought up the rear. They all stopped in the middle of the room, their eyes asking for answers.

"We got married because Daddy found us in that old abandoned dugout down by Bear Creek. We didn't . . ." she said, high color filling her cheeks.

"I will call James tomorrow and he'll take care of an annulment," Everett explained as he came through the back door. "Should be taken care of in a week or so."

"I see. And Carolina?" Emma asked.

"She'll understand," Everett said, confidently.

Emma didn't have the heart to tell Everett that it wouldn't be that way at all. That she'd had several letters from Carolina recently, telling her that she didn't want to live in a backwoods town like Dodsworth, that she would curl up and die without her social life in Atlanta. Carolina had been Emma's friend in Atlanta for years. Emma had been raised in the south. Her mother died many years before, and her father had just recently married again. This time, a younger woman—Eulalie Dulanis, who was Everett's older sister. Emma had been glad that Everett wanted to come to the territory to practice medicine, since Logan County needed another doctor. Her friends, Violet and Orrin Wilde, had built him a small office in town. Right on the very spot where Violet's house had burned to the ground earlier in the summer. But Emma had always wondered just how Carolina would fare out of her environment.

"Well, why did you spend the night with her?" Mary asked. "If you didn't want to get married, why did you? Wouldn't no one make me marry up with a man if I didn't want to."

"Oh, hush," Sarah, the oldest child, piped up. "Ben Listen had a shotgun. Grace said it was a shotgun wedding."

Maggie smiled. Leave it to the kids to tell it just like it was.

"Shotgun weddings aren't really legal," Sarah told Mary in an authoritative voice.

"Yes, they are," Jimmy said. "I heard Ben saying he was taking the license to Guthrie tomorrow so it couldn't be undone."

"Well, I for one am starving," Jed changed the subject. "Why don't you all come on up to the house and we'll fix some lunch?"

"We just ate breakfast," Maggie said. "Just got finished with it and taking a bath to get all the mud off us."

Emma smiled, remembering the tough times she and Jed had in this very cabin back in the beginning of their marriage. Jed's sister and brother-in-law had died of cholera, leaving him their land claim, a cabin, and four kids to raise. Emma's father was insisting that she marry up with some banker down in Atlanta, and she was running from that when she met Jed. They'd married on the spot and it looked like it wouldn't ever work. Her being a rich girl from the south; him just a poor farmer. But it did in the end. And now they had little Lalie Joy.

Maggie read the thoughts on Emma's beautiful face. Well, that was one miracle that wouldn't be repeated just because she and Everett spent a few nights in this cabin. No siree, she wasn't about to stay married to a man who couldn't laugh or dance.

"Well, then we'll get on and leave you two alone. You get lonely, come on up to the house." Jed nodded up the hill toward the big white house with a porch wrapped around three sides.

"Violet said you could stay with her," Emma said just loud enough for Maggie to hear. "We kind of figured that this was the way things went. Ben has just got a temper and Elenor's been eyeballing Ivan Svenson, and moaning about you not ever getting married, so it sure makes it easy on him and your Momma."

"Yes, it does. But I ain't running away from my problems. Everett can sleep in the loft and I'll do what I do all the time at home anyway. Cook, mend, do laundry, clean. When the papers are done, I'm going far away," Maggie said, and smiled.

"Okay, but Violet and I are here for you if you need us," Emma said.

"I know that," Maggie said. "I don't mean to be saying bad things about your relative, Emma. He's a good man. It's just that he ain't no better than Jim Parsons. He's too serious and he doesn't enjoy dancing."

"Come on, Momma," Jimmy yelled from the wagon. "I'm starving."

Everett picked up a medical book he'd been studying and sat down in the rocking chair. Maggie looked delightful in his blue shirt, with his pants roped in at the waist with a green calico sash. Too bad she was so dumb and couldn't carry on a conversation about anything but dancing. He'd have to spend the next week with her; a little intelligent conversation would have been nice.

Maggie went out onto the porch to wait for Elenor. She hoped she didn't forget her comb. Maggie's hair wasn't easy to deal with at best, but when it dried without the use of a good combing it was doubly difficult. She waited two hours, just rocking back and forth in the swing, before her sister drove the wagon into the yard.

"Daddy said for me to bring you this stuff." Elenor's eyes widened in surprise when she saw her sister dressed like a man. "What are you doing wearing that? Daddy will have a fit."

"Daddy finished telling me what to do this morning when he shoved that shotgun in my ribs and made me marry Dr. Everett," Maggie said. "I'll help you unload this. Can you have supper with us?"

"No, I'm going home. I'm not staying here. I'm having enough trouble making Ivan see that I'm not the kind of woman you are," Elenor smarted off. "Momma is mad, too.

Guess you better stay away from our place for a little while."

Maggie walked on tender bare feet to the back of the wagon and began lifting out her things. Her clothing had been haphazardly thrown into her trunk, several pieces still hanging out even though the trunk was closed. She manhandled it onto the porch while Elenor took several more pillow cases stuffed full to the porch. Only one box remained up behind the wagon seat.

"Momma said she didn't even want your old cat to remind her of you right now, so she sent Patches." Elenor brought the box to the porch.

Maggie fell on the box like it was filled with pure gold. "Patches, my pretty baby," she crooned as she pried the lid off with her fingers and brought the big black and white cat out to cuddle it.

"I'm going home now, Maggie. You done made your bed like Daddy said. So you can just make the best of it. Maybe when me and Ivan get married, things will be blowed over and you can come to the wedding." Elenor crawled up in the seat and left without another word.

"I hope so," Maggie whispered so quietly only the wind and the pain inside her soul heard her sweet voice. She buried her face in Patches' black and white fur to keep from actually crying. "I hope you aren't ever as miserable as I am right now, Elenor. I hope you and Ivan fall in love and when he kisses you, the whole world stands still. That's the way it's supposed to be."

Chapter Three

Just before dawn was Everett's favorite time of day. A time when he sat in the rocking chair and watched the sun come up out the front window. A half an hour before all the hustle and bustle of living started. The bed springs rattled in the bedroom where Maggie slept. Even that couldn't bother Everett as he propped his feet on a footstool, laced his hands behind his head, and forced every thought from his mind. Except those of deciding if this morning's sunrise was more beautiful than any other one he'd ever experienced.

Maggie's cat, Patches, sat up in the basket beside the fireplace and stretched. She spent a few minutes washing her face, then hopped out of the basket and rubbed around the table leg a few times. She eyed the man in the rocking chair. It wasn't Maggie's father or that big man who came around once in a while to see Elenor. This male critter looked harmless, but he hadn't offered even once to pet Patches. Finally, she grew weary with her surveillance of the new man and hopped up on the kitchen window sill.

The rattle of a buggy and horse brought Everett out of his quiet time. It wasn't unusual at all for someone to come looking for the country doctor. His hours weren't only from eight to five in his office. If an emergency or a new baby's arrival needed him, then the folks in most of the eastern half of Logan County already knew he lived in Emma and Jed's cabin. He tucked his clean white shirt into his dark trousers, clamped his suspenders to the waistband, and smoothed back his hair with his fingertips. The black bag waited by the door; his jacket and hat both hung on the hat rack; his shoes were right beside Patches' basket. Everything stayed ready so he could be out on his way in no more than two minutes in an emergency. He hoped it wasn't Orrin Wilde coming to tell him that Violet had lost their baby. They were so happy with the prospects of their first child. Violet was less than half way into the pregnancy but so far everything had been going well.

The buggy stopped outside the cabin and he opened the door. The buggy was a hired one from Guthrie with Buffet's Livery written in fancy gold lettering on the side. Dr. Jones usually took care of everything in Guthrie, as well as western Logan County. He'd been relieved that Everett set up practice in Dodsworth. Said he was getting too old to take care of the whole area. So why would anyone from Guthrie be hunting for Everett? He leaned against the door and waited for his answer. A tall man with a shock of white hair circled the buggy from the rear and helped a lady down. The two of them were almost to the porch when Everett realized in the semi-darkness of the early dawn just who had arrived.

Carolina Prescott and her father! Holy smoke. His Carolina in Dodsworth on a surprise visit. A smile covered his handsome face and he stepped out of the doorway with open arms. Carolina carefully avoided his arms and held her hand out to him instead. He bent low over it and kissed the palm of the hand where his engagement ring was supposed to be. She must have forgotten to put it on this morning.

"My darling, what a wonderful surprise. Why didn't you write? I would have met the train and secured lodging for you closer than Guthrie." Everett was afraid to blink. His precious, sweet Carolina right before his eyes.

"We really need to talk," Carolina said softly. "Daddy and I have to be back in Guthrie by ten o'clock this morning to catch our train to Philadelphia."

"But why are you going to Philadelphia? You didn't mention anything about a trip in your last letter. Please come inside. I'll make a pot of tea and we'll visit," he said, opening the door and letting them enter before him.

Carolina's nose snarled at the sight of the small cabin. She'd seen squatter's cabins in Georgia just like this. Tiny little hovels overrun with snotty nosed kids with no shoes, and hound dogs living under the front porch. The only difference was that someone had at least painted this one white and planted some common old zinnias around the porch. The inside wasn't a lot better: one big room with a fireplace at one end and a kitchen at the other. It looked clean and orderly but she'd expect that much from Everett. A ladder led up to what looked like a bedroom loft, and then there were two doors. One to a bedroom and one outside, she guessed. Her suite of rooms on the second floor of the plantation was twice as big as this squalid little place. If she had any misgivings about the decisions she'd made in the past few weeks, they dissolved when she looked at the homemade hooked rugs thrown about on the rough wood floors. How in the world had Emma ever lived in such abject poverty?

"How have you been, Mr. Prescott? Please forgive my rudeness in not addressing you. I was so surprised at seeing you two." Everett fumbled with the match to start the fire in the stove.

"I've been fine, Everett. No offense taken, I'm sure. Don't bother making tea. We really don't have time for it, anyway. I'm going to wait in the buggy and give you time to talk. Carolina. Fifteen minutes?" He raised an eyebrow. Thank goodness his daughter had come to her senses before it was too late. He couldn't bear the thought of her ever living in this absolute wilderness. Everett had written that he was designing a proper home for her so she wouldn't have had to live in this cabin very long. That Mr. Prescott would have forbidden, even for a week, since he'd seen the place. Until Everett had the house finished he would not have given his daughter in marriage to the man. At least he didn't have to worry about such a decision now. The stark reality of Carolina coming so close to living in such a primitive area was enough to make him shudder.

"I'll be ready." Carolina smoothed the front of her deep blue traveling skirt. The matching jacket was cut of the same material but the bow at the top of her hips in the back was black velvet, matching the trim on her hat and the gloves she held in her right hand.

The minute her father was out the door, Everett crossed the room in four easy strides and took Carolina in his arms. Just a few minutes. Lord, that wasn't even long enough for him to tell her how beautiful she looked, how he dreamed about her every night, how much he missed her, or how he wanted to hold her in his arms forever. "Oh, my darling," he said with a sigh.

"I have something to return to you, Everett. I don't know how to tell you this. But I felt like I had to do it in person rather than by letter. It's hard for me to do, however, I'm glad I decided to do it this way. Now I've seen Oklahoma and I know I've made the right decisions," she said, pushing her way out of his embrace and walking to the front door.

"Carolina, whatever are you talking about?" A cold chill started at the base of his spine and traveled slowly to his scalp, where a prickly sensation made his dark hair stand on end. Something definitely was wrong. Carolina never treated him like this. She'd been enamored with him from the first time they met—at Eulalie and Jefferson's engagement party.

"Everett, how determined are you to stay in this forsaken

place? Will you reconsider and live in New York again or even Atlanta?" she asked, her blue eyes never wavering.

He'd never heard such a cold edge to her voice. "I told you why I wanted to move here. We discussed it, Carolina. I want to make a difference in people's lives. I want to be a part of this new state. I love it here. The sunrises are almost as breathtaking as you are. The people are friendly and nice. They need me. New York doesn't need me. There's a doctor on every street corner. Are you telling me that you hate Oklahoma, when you've barely seen it and met none of the kind people? Are you saying that you won't live here?"

"That's what I'm saying," she said.

"But you said you loved me," he said.

"I don't love anyone or anything enough to live in this kind of place," she said flatly.

Before he could answer, hinges squeaked as Maggie pushed open the bedroom door. She wore a long, faded mint green nightgown, and her strange colored, dark red hair fell in a tangle of loose curls and waves all the way to her hips. Bare feet peeked out from the flounce ruffle at the hem of the gown. She rubbed the sleep from her eyes, expecting to see no one but maybe Patches up so early.

"Who are you?" Carolina demanded shrilly, pointing with one delicate finger.

"Oh, my. I thought I'd be the only one awake this early," Maggie stammered.

"I didn't ask you that. I asked who are you?" Carolina demanded.

"I'm Maggie, ma'am. Who are you?" Maggie had the feeling she'd just stepped into a witch's brewing pot. Though the woman was dressed like one of those women in a fancy magazine, rage colored her face and evil shot from her eyes as she stared at Maggie. In spite of the look on her face, her outfit was absolutely beautiful, and lovely was the lady. Blonde hair arranged just perfect under that cute little hat. Maggie felt every bit of the country bumpkin standing there in her old worn flannel nightgown with her hair all messy from sleep and her face not even washed. Her feet wouldn't move but her heart and soul wanted to run back into the bedroom and slam the door.

"What are you doing here?" Carolina's high-pitched voice raised both in timbre and volume.

"Well, it's a long story but Everett and I got married," Maggie stammered.

"Married?" Carolina turned toward Everett. She drew back her dainty little hand and slapped his face, leaving an imprint that would go with him most of the morning.

"I can explain, Carolina," Everett said. "For goodness sake, Maggie, go back in the bedroom and put on some clothes."

Carolina? Mercy! What was she doing in Dodsworth? Better yet, what was she doing here before daylight? Maggie wondered as her green eyes widened at the red print on Everett's face. He certainly didn't deserve that kind of treatment. This whole horrible situation wasn't any more his fault than it was hers.

"No," Carolina screamed again. "Don't you go anywhere. You stay right there, you trollop. Here's what I brought you back." She pulled his diamond engagement ring from her reticule and tossed it at his feet.

"Wait a minute." Maggie's temper was rising fast enough to rival Carolina's. "You wait a minute. This is not what it looks like. It was a shotgun wedding. My daddy got the wrong idea because we were forced to spend the night together in an old abandoned house. We didn't do anything, but we had to take off our wet clothes or die of pneumonia. Now sit your bottom down on that chair and listen to sense. This marriage ain't a marriage and we are going to undo it. You can go ahead and have him if you want him. It's just that you got to wait for the papers to be fixed to undo this mess. And don't call me a trollop. You don't even know me. I'm not a tramp. And don't you never hit Everett again, this ain't his fault." Maggie figured if she was going to be a contestant in a cat fight she'd better bare her claws and get ready for battle.

"I'll call you what I please." Carolina glared at the woman who'd most certainly spent the night in Everett's bed the night before.

If looks could kill, Maggie would have dropped in nothing but a heap of flannel and dark red hair. "Sit down and listen to sense." Maggie pulled a chair out from the table. "If I was you, I'd probably be pretty mad too. But you don't have to give back his ring. This isn't a real marriage. And it'll be all took care of in a few days."

"I'm leaving. I came here to do the dignified thing, Everett Jackson Dulanis. I won't marry you. I couldn't stand to live in this kind of squalor," Carolina snapped at Everett and ignored Maggie. The woman was crazy if she thought for one minute Carolina would believe a word she said. Actions spoke louder than words, and what appeared to happen was more important than the facts. That's what her southern bred mother always said, and Carolina realized the wisdom in the words right then in the middle of this squatter's cabin in Oklahoma.

"I've already hired a crew to build you a home," he said. His heart lay at his feet, a pulsating lump of pain and pure humiliation.

"I don't care. Even if it's bigger than my plantation, I still couldn't stand to live here anyway. No social life at all, Everett. And people like that to be friends with." She nodded her head toward Maggie. "No thank you. Daddy and I are on the way to Philadelphia. We made the trip through here so I could break it off with you. I didn't know that it wasn't necessary since you've already chosen one of these needy people over me. Stay married to her," she said, pointing at Maggie like she was something she'd just wiped off her expensive boots.

"Oh, no, honey." Maggie shook her head. "I don't want him. Never did. If he can't laugh or dance, then he's not for Maggie."

"But he can. He can dance with the best of them." Carolina turned to stare him right in the eye. "And laugh. Of course he can laugh. He's been laughing at me ever since he came to this horrid place. Laughing so hard at the southern lady whose eyes he's pulling the wool over. I'm going. Eulalie sends her best, by the way. She's sorry things couldn't work out and that you feel so drawn to a life in this place. She told me you were stubborn and wouldn't change your mind, but I didn't think you were stupid, too, Everett." Carolina opened the door. "Good-bye. Oh, I guess it doesn't matter now. You're already married. So it won't break your little heart to know that I'm going to Philadelphia to accept the proposal of another doctor. I'd planned on breaking that news to you later, when you'd had time to heal from the shock of losing my love. But that isn't important now. Maybe you'll remember him. He was your best friend in New York. You brought him to Atlanta last summer. Gatlin O'Malley. He plans to set up a practice in Atlanta so I don't have to leave my friends and family."

Everett's feet were glued to the spot on the floor as tightly as his tongue was glued to the roof of his mouth. He was speechless. His heart was broken, his soul ripped in two halves, his whole world torn apart in the course of fifteen minutes.

Maggie's heart went out to Everett. She might not like the man, but no one deserved the treatment that hussy was giving him. The bewildered look on his face made her want to at least give him a sisterly hug. The smug, hateful look on Carolina's face caused Maggie to clasp her hands behind her back to keep from thrashing the woman.

Carolina played the little tableau to the hilt, holding her chin high, fluttering her eyelashes and letting the hint of a condescending smile play at the corners of her bow-shaped mouth. Everett was much more handsome than Gatlin; but good looks wouldn't be worth anything in this place. Gatlin, bless his heart, had revealed his attraction for her just a couple of weeks ago, saying that he'd fallen in love with her but he wouldn't hurt his friend Everett for anything. Several clandestine visits later, she'd convinced him that she wasn't going to marry Everett anyway.

Patches watched a robin and wished she was outside rather than sitting in the room with all these crazy human people. She could have had that fat robin for breakfast. She hopped off the ledge and started toward the door just about the same time a mouse peeked around the backside of her basket. Well, if a robin couldn't be had, then a mouse would have to do. Her whiskers twitched as she made a hoarse sound in her throat. She slinked behind the wide skirts of the new woman critter who had arrived a while ago and never had sat down to make a lap for her to have a nap in. The mouse wasn't even aware she was near.

"Good-bye, Everett," Carolina said again as she turned.

When she did, the mouse saw the cat and ran to the nearest shelter which was under all those wide blue skirts. Patches dove at the mouse, sweeping a set of claws at the hem of the skirt. Carolina screamed and began some kind of fancy footwork as the mouse climbed right up her finest lace trimmed drawers. The cat made her way through all that material and under the petticoats. Her breakfast was getting away by climbing right up the lady's legs. She sat still and watched patiently. When the stupid critter reached the top, there was no way to go but back down—then she'd simply grab him with her well-sharpened claws. That is, if the crazy woman would stop stomping around. One thing for sure, if that fool stepped on her tail in amongst all that carrying on, she intended to climb right up all that white lace and fetch that mouse before he came down.

"I hate cats—hate mice!" Carolina screamed again, which brought her father storming through the front door.

"What on earth are you doing to my daughter?" he demanded.

"Not one thing," Everett whispered.

"Would you stop this caterwauling?" Maggie was suddenly across the room and on her knees, pulling a reluctant Patches from under the skirt tails.

The terrified mouse took advantage of the situation and ran down the back side of Carolina's legs and out from her skirt to hide behind the leg of the stove. Patches let out a loud meow and jumped from Maggie's arms to continue the chase. The poor mouse tried to outrun her but the chase ended at the back door when a hungry Patches caught it. She was too hungry to play with it or even take it to Maggie to brag about her conquest. She just flopped down on her fat belly and commenced to eating it, tail first.

"Oh, yuk." Carolina pressed the back of her hand to her forehead. "Daddy, get me out of this filth."

"Yes, my dear." Mr. Prescott slipped his arm around Carolina's waist. She was entirely too delicate for this. "Who are you?" He looked back at the bedraggled red-haired woman who didn't seem the least bit offended by the cat.

"I am Everett's wife," Maggie said. She'd save him a bit of dignity. He had, of course, married her instead of taking the shotgun shells between his eyes. That southern piece of over-rated baggage could just go marry that Gatlin fellow. But she didn't need to think she broke Everett's heart doing so.

"You are who?" Mr. Prescott stopped in his tracks and glared at Everett.

"I can explain, sir," Everett said.

"I don't need an explanation. I'm taking Carolina to Philadelphia where she will announce her engagement to the man who will take care of her proper. I should call you out for a duel for this, Dulanis," he said.

"Daddy, don't. Just get me out of here. I never want to see this place again," Carolina said.

"Yes, my child," he said. "I can't believe you'd take that hoyden to bed rather than honoring your promise to my daughter. Well, you've made your bed, Everett Dulanis. Now you can just live in this nasty place with your ugly, plain wife, knowing every day what you threw away to have it."

"But, sir." Everett stepped to the door as they left. "There's an explanation. I don't want you to think I've been dishonorable."

"Daddy, please," Carolina said, dragging his arm toward the buggy. "Don't take the time to listen to his lies."

"Good-bye. You don't know what honorable is." Mr. Prescott seated her and drove away, leaving nothing but a beautiful sunrise in his wake.

Maggie suddenly felt like just what Carolina's father had called her. Plain and ugly. Standing there beside her cat who'd just polished off the last of a mouse and was licking her paws, she wanted to run away and never look back. She'd never be a beauty like Carolina. But that man had no right to treat her like she was someone's slave. The slaves had been set free years ago, and even they didn't get that kind of disrespect anymore. Tears welled up in her eyes—but she wouldn't shed them. Everett didn't need a bawling wife after what he'd just been through. Even if he wasn't funny and couldn't dance all the country dances she knew perfectly, he wasn't dishonorable. He was the most honorable man she'd ever met. Marrying her. Giving her the bedroom. Bragging on her biscuits.

That thought reminded her of why she'd come out of the bedroom in her night rail anyway. "I'll get your breakfast ready now," she said, surprised that her voice came out normal sounding.

"I'm not hungry. I'm going into Guthrie. I want to be there when the telegram office opens so I can send a note to my lawyer," he said coldly.

"Hey, don't blame me because your sweet little honey turned out to be an idiot. I told you when you tried to hire me to cook for her that she wouldn't see things the way you thought she would. She's just a woman—and a hateful one at that," she snapped.

"Carolina is a sensitive woman. She couldn't bear the

thought of my betrayal. She was probably just making up that story about Gatlin. He's my good friend. He wouldn't do that to me," Everett said, as he put on his shoes and tied them in neat bows.

"Don't bet on it, honey." Maggie clenched her hands into tight little balls at her sides.

Everett slipped on his coat and picked up his bag. He'd walk the half mile up to Emma and Jed's. They'd said yesterday he could use their buggy until his was repaired. His horse had been found in the pasture nibbling on grass when they got home from the church the day before, so he wouldn't need to borrow one of theirs. Was it really just yesterday morning that he'd awakened with the shotgun pressed to his forehead?

"Don't you walk out that door without your breakfast," Maggie said.

"You are not my wife. You never will be. You might want a man who can dance and make you laugh. Well, I want a wife who is refined and dignified, who will be a helpmate for me in my profession. You, lady, are about as qualified for that job as a sow in a wallow. I'm going to Guthrie. I'll be home in time for supper. When this horrible experience is finished, I will pay you for your duties taking care of my home and cooking for me. Hopefully, you will take it and disappear from my life forever," Everett said levelly but coldly.

"You're going to beg that witch for another chance, aren't you? Well, it won't do you a bit of good, Everett Dulanis. She wasn't lying about that Gatlin fellow. And she won't live here either. She looked at this cabin like it was the filthiest heap in the territory. It's a nice place, Everett. And if she can't love you for the good man you are, then she don't deserve you. I won't take your money, either. I live here too, you know. I can see how you feel about me, it's written all over your face. But it don't matter, because when the papers are finished, I'm going far away.

I don't want to see you again, either." Maggie bit the inside of her lip.

Everett just set his jaw and walked out the door.

The crack of the slamming door along with the deafening blast of silence brought on the tears. They streamed down her face and dripped onto her gown. Ugly. Plain. A fat old sow in a wallow. Add stupid to that, since he didn't think she could carry on a conversation about anything other than dances and fun. There wasn't a fragment of Maggie's pride left in the little cabin as she sobbed into her drawn up knees.

Patches, her tummy now full of fresh mouse, saw a shiny thing on the floor. She was in the mood for a good tummy rub, but Maggie wasn't laughing or calling her to come and sit in her lap. The shiny thing on the floor captured her attention. She wiggled and squirmed to see if it would run across the floor. She laid her belly low and slinked along the wooden floor until she could touch it. She bared her claws and dragged the sparkling round thing to her side, scraping it across the wooden floor as she did so. Maggie raised her swollen red eyes to see what made the noise.

"Give me that." She took it away from Patches, held it up to the new morning light, and let the sparkles from the big diamond dance in front of her eyes. Tears filled her eyes again; tears even shinier than the diamond streaked down her cheeks.

"You foolish woman. He loved you. Do you know what I'd give for a man to love me like he does you? I'd worship him. But I won't ever have that kind of love because I'm just plain old Maggie, who ain't smart," she said, standing up.

She gently laid the ring on the kitchen table and went back to her bedroom to get dressed. Today was Monday. Plain, ugly, pretty, rich, or poor, there was a washing to do.

Chapter Four

A warm Indian summer caused sweat to pop out on Maggie's forehead. She mopped it away with the back of her hand. It was her own fault that the sun beat down on her head and the hot air cooked her pale skin. She'd forgotten her bonnet when she stormed out of the cabin. Now Everett could add *freckled* to the list of ugly things he said about his new wife. He could also include the word *gone,* because that's exactly what she intended to be by daylight the next day. It would be a hot day in January when she ever thought about really getting married if this was what it was like.

"Men!" she said disgustedly, as she lifted the full skirt of her faded blue checked dress to keep from getting the hem muddy. "No wonder married women go around with long faces and sigh so often." *What about Emma and Violet?* Her conscience pricked her red hot anger.

"Emma and Violet are a different story. They got good men. Men that love them. That's what I wanted; but I sure enough didn't get it. Not with a shotgun for a maid of honor. And now that my name has been drug through the mud worse than my skirt tails, I won't ever have it. No decent man would want a woman with a history like mine." She stomped along the dirt road toward town. Married one day. Separated the next. Maybe divorced before the week was over. The only way to get a worse name was if she went to Guthrie and got a job as a barmaid in one of the saloons over there. She almost smiled at that thought. It would be good enough for her father if she did just that. At least she could dance every night and wear shiny satin dresses. The whole county was going to disown her anyway. She shrugged away the idea when she reached town. Not even when she was angry could Maggie take a job like that.

The sign said *Dr. Everett Dulanis, M.D.* and it squeaked as the breeze blew it gently back and forth on the hinges. Emma had ordered it made especially for Everett and they'd had a bit of a town celebration when he hung it up the first time. There had been a welcoming picnic and he'd made a speech. The one thing Maggie remembered was that he'd told them he wasn't standing on formality, to please call him Dr. Everett. Had someone told Maggie Listen that day that she would be married to the man before the fall leaves fell from the scrub oak trees she would have thought they had cow chips for brains.

The squeak of the new sign along with the violent retching of someone at the edge of the porch losing their lunch in the yellow rose bushes quickly got Maggie's attention. She stomped her foot extra hard. Was nothing ever going to go right again? He had a patient, and a sick one at that. She'd figured he'd either be alone in his office or else out on a call, in which case she'd just sit on the porch and wait. All she wanted was a few quiet moments with Everett to tell him that even this arrangement wasn't going to work. If he'd simply take her to Guthrie she'd try to find a job. She couldn't go home and had enough pride that she didn't want to live with either of her good friends, Violet Wilde or Emma Thomas.

"Anna Marie?" Maggie stopped on the porch. Anna Marie, the preacher's daughter, was the one leaning over the rose bushes and hugging the porch railing like it was a long lost friend. A couple of years before, Anna Marie had married the banker, Alford Manor, from over in Guthrie. They had a small son and another baby on the way. "Are you all right?" Maggie asked.

"It's little Alford. He's cut his foot on a fruit jar and there was blood and oh, Maggie, it made me so sick just to look at it," Anna Marie said.

Maggie almost felt sorry for her. The woman had a tongue sharper than Granny Listen's butcher knife and wasn't one bit bashful when it came to speaking her mind. There was a time when she had her sights set for Jed Thomas, Emma's husband, and said some pretty hateful things about Emma. Then there was the scandal when Orrin got shot and Violet took care of him. It might not have looked so good in the proper society of Dodsworth for Orrin to live right in the house with the widow McDonald, but that didn't give Anna Marie the right to say the mean things she did. Not to mention all the times she'd been snide to Maggie. Still, Maggie's heart went out to the petite woman who was now being sick again over the edge of the porch. After all, her baby was hurt, and that would be hard on a proper lady like Anna Marie.

The baby in question let out a scream that would have curled the hair on Lucifer's beard about then. Maggie heard the agitation in Everett's voice as he tried desperately to talk the year-old child into letting him look at the wound.

"Sit down on the porch and put your head between your knees and don't look up until your stomach has stopped retching," Maggie told Anna Marie.

"I can't do that. What if someone came by and saw me?" Anna Marie clamped her hand over her mouth, a faint green shade deepening around her lips.

"I'd worry more about the roses you're destroying," Maggie said. "Do what I say and forget about what people think, Anna Marie. You aren't so fat yet that you can't get your head between your knees. Sit on the porch and take deep breaths. I'm going in to help with little Alford. Don't you come in there no matter what."

"I won't." Anna Marie slid down onto the porch and dutifully laid her head on her propped up knees. "If I did I'm sure I'd faint dead away on the floor."

Maggie nodded, then threw open the door into the doctor's office. Little Alford was on the examination table, screaming at the top of his lungs. His wispy blonde hair was wet with sweat. His eyes were round, not with fear but pure old unadulterated rage. He was truly his mother's son. Blood dripped through the kitchen towel Anna Marie had wound around his foot, and the baby had it smeared all over his face, his snowy white dress, and his legs.

Everett was a picture of exasperation. If Maggie hadn't been so upset with him and his pompous, over-inflated ego, she might have felt sorry for him. But she'd used up all her pity on Anna Marie.

"I'm glad you are here. Can you hold him down so I can look at this wound? I know it's going to require stitches, but his mother can't help me and there's no way I can do something as intricate as sew up a baby's tender foot without some help," Everett asked stiffly.

Maggie nodded. "Okay, little Alford," she said, turning to the baby and speaking in a no-nonsense voice. "Hush that caterwauling right now."

The noise stopped immediately and the baby stared at her in bewilderment. No one had ever used that tone of voice at him before in his life. Usually if he bawled, he got whatever he wanted. And he wanted to go back to his Granny's house and play with the kittens. He didn't want the strange man to touch his foot.

"Now Dr. Everett is going to look at your foot and you're going to be still." Maggie sat down beside him on the examining table. "If you scream and carry on, I'm going to hold you down and he's going to do it anyway."

"No," Little Alford said, his pretty mouth a perfect O.

"Yes," Maggie said. "But if you lay very still and don't

make a sound, when the doctor is finished, me and you will go to the store and you can have a candy stick."

"Candy?" His eyes glittered.

"Go ahead," Maggie said with a nod toward Everett.

"No," Little Alford screamed.

"Okay," Maggie said, holding her hands up to the child. "I'll take it off and we'll look at it together.

Everett figured he'd have to catch Maggie when she fainted at the sight of the bloody wound. That's all he needed to round out a horrid day. A screaming child on the examining table and a woman at his feet. When she unwound the towel and saw a gaping cut still dripping blood, she'd faint or vomit. He didn't have time for either one. No woman could look at a bloody wound like that and not turn six shades of green. Look at the child's mother out there making a nasty mess of his yellow rose bushes. He crossed his arms and waited. Talk about a day from the bowels of Hades. This had been it. First the fiasco with Carolina at daybreak. Then the argument with Maggie and the absolutely horrid ride to Guthrie over muddy roads. Not to even mention the next heartbreaker at the train station. And now this spoiled child.

She removed the towel and reached out to the basin of water Everett had ready at the side of the table. She picked up the clean white cloth and gently washed the drying blood away from the wound. The water in the basin turned scarlet as she dipped the rag in several times but when she finished everything but the gaping wound was clean. "I think you can see it good enough now."

"No," Little Alford screamed again when the doctor took a step toward him.

"It needs about three stitches to heal properly." Everett looked but didn't touch. "It's going to sting, and . . ."

"I will hold him down. He's going to scream, but I would, too. And he's just a baby. We're the big people. I'm strong enough to keep him still. You just take care of the cut," she said.

"Can you do it?" Everett was still amazed that she was standing and not outside with Anna Marie.

The daggers Maggie shot at him would have felled an elephant if they'd been real, but her eyes softened when she turned back to the child. "Okay, child, this is going to hurt. I ain't going to lie to you, baby, but it's necessary." She held him by the shoulders and forced him to look at her. It was as if he found comfort down in the depths of her mossy green eyes.

Everett mixed something in a basin of clean water and Maggie's nose began to twitch. It was a stronger version of the strange smell permeating his whole office. Could be that Anna Marie wasn't so sick because of the sight of blood but because of that odd odor.

"What is that?" she asked.

"An antiseptic to clean the wound. We've found that it reduces gangrene by at least seventy-five percent," he said flatly.

The baby began to cry—not tears of rage now, but of pain. Maggie's heart went out to the little fellow. Misbehaved and rambunctious as he was, it was a shame for babies to ever suffer. There was enough of that in store for them when they were adults.

"Okay, I'm ready to begin," Everett said.

"I'm going to lay right down here beside you and hold you tight so it won't hurt so bad," Maggie said crawling up on the bed with the child and gathering him up tightly in her arms. He buried his face in her bosom and sobbed. She raised her skirt tail and secured his chubby leg with hers, holding it in a vice grip so the doctor could sew the wound shut. She felt his small leg jerk when the first needles went into the very sweet, tender skin of his foot. Tears filled her eyes, but from her mouth came soothing words to little Alford as the doctor concentrated on his job.

"All finished with that part. Now I'm bandaging," Everett said.

It had only taken a few minutes, according to the clock

hanging on the wall of his office, but it was only a few seconds short of eternity for Maggie. She cooed and told him what a brave little boy he'd been—but she didn't turn him loose. Not yet. Not until it was all finished.

"Now one more little job. If you can hold his arm steady, Maggie. He needs a tetanus shot," Everett said.

"A what?" Maggie couldn't believe the child would have to put up with anything else. Surely this poor little thing had endured enough for one day.

"It's something new and very effective. It's called a tetanus injection. Just a little something I'll put in his arm. It'll sting and he'll probably cry some more." Everett pulled medicine from a large bottle into a syringe and Maggie shuddered. Just the thought of being poked with that needle was enough to turn her stomach as much as the sight of blood.

"Why?" she asked.

"It will keep him from getting lockjaw." Everett used the common term for the dreaded disease. "When something foreign enters the body, like a rusty nail or what could have been on that dirty fruit jar, it sets up infection and causes lockjaw. This will keep him from getting it."

"Then hurry up." Maggie clamped his arm tightly and smothered his wet little cheeks with kisses.

Little Alford didn't even tense when the needle pierced his skin; but Maggie did. "I'm so sorry, baby. It'll get well and you won't even remember it at all, not at your age."

"Finished." Everett breathed a sigh of relief.

"Candy?" The baby smiled at Maggie.

"All you want, sweetheart," Maggie picked him up gently. "Do you have an account at the general store?"

"Yes, I do," Everett said with a nod.

"Then we are going to buy candy. We'll be back in a few minutes." She patted his back as they walked out onto the porch. "We're going for candy because he was so good," she said to Anna Marie, who retched again when she saw blood on little Alford's dress.

"Get a hold of yourself, girl. He don't need to see you like that," Maggie said stiffly.

"What you got there?" Duncan, the store owner, asked when he looked up from his books and saw Maggie. "Heard you got married yesterday but didn't know even you could produce a baby that fast." He chuckled at his own joke.

"It's little Alford. He stepped on a broken fruit jar and Dr. Everett had to sew him up. It hurt like the thunder and he's going to have a candy stick. Matter of fact, I want that whole jar of candy sticks."

"Well, Maggie, that would be a whole dollar. There's a hundred sticks in a jar and I just put the jar out this morning. Ain't nobody even opened it yet," Duncan said.

"Put it on the doctor's bill." She shifted Alford to her right hip and picked up the jar of candy.

"Yes, ma'am." Duncan smiled. "Now tell me what's this story about you getting married?"

"No story. Dr. Everett and I got married. Don't know how long it might last but we are married today, Duncan, and today is all we got." Maggie started out of the store, a baby on one hip reaching for candy and the other arm firmly wrapped around a large jar of peppermint candy sticks.

"Can he dance?" Duncan asked.

"'Bout like a bear with two left feet," Maggie tossed over her shoulder as she opened the screen door.

"Then why'd you marry him?" Duncan called out.

"Because my daddy had a shotgun and he said I would," Maggie said honestly.

The doctor's office was less than a block away but little Alford got heavier and heavier. Anna Marie paled again when she raised an eyebrow and looked at the blood on his dress. "Just sit still and I'll take it off him," Maggie said. Mercy, when she had children was she going to act like that?

She kicked the door open with the toe of her shoe and sat the baby on the examining table. His dirty hands reached toward the jar. "Candy," he said loudly and puckered up to cry.

"Hush," Maggie said firmly. "You can have your candy but first we got to get the blood all off you or else your Momma won't be able to take you home." Maggie talked as she washed the dried blood from his face, hands, hair, and legs. "Now let's get you out of that dress. Well, glory be, your undershirt doesn't have anything on it. She can take you home in that. And now, my pretty boy, you can have your candy. You can reach right down in that jar and get it yourself." She twisted the lid off the jar.

"You think you bought enough?" Everett came in from the store room where he kept his supplies.

"From now on you keep this candy jar in full sight of any child who comes in here. No matter what that child needs done, he's to have a candy stick when you get done. It will make your job easier," Maggie said shortly.

"But a whole jar?" he argued. Drat the woman anyway. Making decisions like that. *You should have thought of it before now. It makes good common sense,* he thought.

"And when that one is empty, you buy another one," she said. "Now, sweetheart, I think I've got you cleaned up enough so we won't have to take you to your momma's funeral if she looks at you." She gathered the squirmy child up in her arms and gave him one final hug before she went back outside.

Everett followed her to the door. Perhaps he'd better check Anna Marie. Even if she wasn't his patient, she'd been violently ill and she was pregnant. That, and he did need to tell her how to care for the wound.

"He's ready to go home," Maggie announced cheerfully. "I kept his little dress and the towel. I'll wash them out and bring them to church next Sunday."

"Oh, my baby!" Anna Marie grabbed the child and held him close to her breast.

"The cut required three stitches. Not a big cut, but deep," Everett said. "I gave him a tetanus injection, so his arm will be sore also. The tetanus is to prevent lockjaw. Keep the wound on his foot dry and clean. If at all possible, don't let him walk on it. Take him in to see Dr. Jones tomorrow. And I'm sure he'll want to take the stitches out in about ten days."

"Thank you, Dr. Everett," Anna Marie said stiffly.

"And here's a candy stick for you," Maggie held out a red and white stick of peppermint to Anna Marie. "It'll settle your stomach. You don't need to be losing your dinner in your condition."

"In my condition!" Anna Marie turned toward Maggie. "Well, who are you to say that to me, Maggie Listen. I'm sorry . . . Maggie Dulanis." She dragged out the last word like it was pure dirt. "I'd say that was the kettle calling the pot black. In my condition. Well, you're in the same condition, or else Ben Listen wouldn't have had my daddy marry you with the doctor. A shotgun wedding, Daddy said. Well, that's the only way you'd ever get a husband, dumb as you are. Guess you finally figured it out for yourself, though, didn't you?"

"Eat the candy, Anna Marie," Maggie said, tiredness creeping into her voice. "It might sweeten up your sour spirit as well as your mouth."

"I really don't think you understand this situation," Dr. Everett said firmly.

"Oh, I understand," Anna Marie snapped. "I understand real well. She can dance but she's stupid. She'll embarrass you and drag you down in Dodsworth until you don't have a good name anymore. I'll send my husband around to pay for your services."

Anna Marie stuck her pretty nose in the air and left a veil of tension surrounding both Maggie and Everett as she pranced down the street. She stopped in front of the general store and threw the candy stick on the wood sidewalk, ground it into a pulp with the heel of her shoe while the baby screamed and reached for it, and looked back over her shoulder to make sure Maggie saw the whole show.

"Whew, talk about a witch." Everett whistled through his teeth.

"That's just Anna Marie," Maggie said. "I think she and your fiancée were cut from the same bolt of cloth. Did you see her in Guthrie?"

Everett bristled. "I told you this morning that was none of your business and I do not intend to discuss it with you. I do want to thank you for your assistance in there, though. I was at my wit's end. Usually some member of the family helps take care of situations like that."

Some member of your family did, she thought. But Everett Dulanis wouldn't ever think of her as his wife. Not when he was forced to marry her. Not even now that she'd come to his rescue. Never.

"It's closing time. You can ride home with me," Everett said.

"I came to tell you that I'm leaving. No need in staying around when you can't abide the sight of someone as ugly as I am, not to mention how dumb. If you'll take me back to the cabin to get my stuff, you can take me to Guthrie. I'll find a job doing something, and when the papers come I'll sign them." Maggie held her head high, but a deep ache split her heart in half.

Everett's own heart chastised him severely. Even if she had caused all kinds of problems, she was a human being, one with feelings. And he'd been a crass fool that morning. *Morning nothing,* he thought. He'd had a mean spirit about her all day; even let Anna Marie get away with being hateful to her. Was this the way the woman had always been treated?

"We're both tired. We've had a really bad day," he said. "Let's go home, eat some supper, and discuss this then."

"Why? You don't want to be married to me. Anna Marie was right. Everyone in Logan County will say you ain't so smart if you married me. If I go away real quick like, they'll forget about it in a few weeks, and you can get your Carolina back. She's not any better than Anna Marie, but she's the kind of wife folks expect you to have. They'll tolerate her just like they always have Anna Marie."

"Maggie, you are not stupid or dumb. I don't know when or where you got that reputation, but it's not true. I'm too tired to discuss this today. Please, let's just go home," he said. "Nothing could be worse than yesterday and today."

"I can say amen to that," she said. He'd said she wasn't dumb. Could it possibly be true that she was as bright as other women? The question reeled in her mind like a ride on a bucking bronco. "I've got a pot of beans on the stove and cornbread made. Figured even if you did take me to Guthrie, you'd need to eat supper. I guess we might as well go eat them. We'll decide on a full stomach what we can do about all this. In a few days, you can go on with your plans for a wedding in Georgia."

Everett gave an ever so brief nod. Carolina wasn't his to be had anymore. She'd made that infinitely clear when he caught up with her at the train station. Even when he explained the situation with Maggie, she'd still been as cold as New York in January. No, he had no notion that things would ever be right in that area again. Maggie had simply fueled the fire that had already been burning. Maggie had been right when she said that Gatlin was really going to marry Carolina. Her father assured him that it was the truth several times. Mr. Prescott had commiserated with him in his sad tale of woe about marrying Maggie with a shotgun present, and agreed that poor Everett had no other alternative but to do the honorable thing. But Carolina was going to Philadelphia to announce her engagement to Gatlin. Everett's spirit was lower than it had ever been in his entire life.

Maggie sat in the buggy while he locked the door to his office. Apparently, he really had gone straight to the train station, and he and Carolina had patched up their engagement after all. Maggie wondered what he'd do with the ring on the table at the cabin? Would he keep it for her—or had he promised her a bigger one when the annulment was final. When God made Alford Manor and Everett Dulanis he surely must have used the same mold, because they were alike in their taste for pretty women. Pretty to look at, but mean as a rattle snake on the inside. If birds of a feather and snakes with the same color skins really did flock together, then Anna Marie and Carolina would be best friends when Everett finally brought her back to Dodsworth to live with him in whatever kind of big house he was planning to build her. Maggie wondered why it was that some men fell in love with such shrewish women? No answers came floating down from the white puffy clouds in the blue skies, though.

Chapter Five

The humidity was high and sweat trickled down James Beauchamp's neck, soaking the stiff collar of his white shirt. The telegram he'd received the day before lay on his desk. Rereading it brought a smile to his round, baby face. He and Everett Jackson Dulanis had been in school together in Terrebonne County, Louisiana, both of them so smart the teacher had trouble keeping up with them. Evidently his good friend had lost some ground in the past few months, because the trouble he'd found himself sure didn't bespeak itself of intelligence.

James needed a vacation from the city, but he had to take care of his friend's problem first. He took a large tome of a book from behind a glassed door and opened it. Just as he thought, it was a thin line—a very skinny one, that left a lot tangled up in his hands. He lit a cigar and paced the floor.

Granny Beauchamp had had *the sight* in her day. He'd asked her about it when he was a child. Did a great thing happen when she saw the future? Did she see visions like dreams only she wasn't sleeping? "No, it's not like that at all," she'd said in a voice barely above a whisper. "It's more like a feeling down deep in your soul that tells you when something needs further study. When you think on it or look deeply into it, then you find the answers, and that's the vision, my child. It's nothing so very mysterious, except for that first gut feeling."

James had a gut feeling, his first ever. And he was just past thirty years old. Had he inherited it from Granny when she passed on last year? If so, this was the first time he needed it. He could prepare the papers and send them to the Indian Territory. Everett and his new bride could sign them in front of a judge and file them in the Logan County courthouse. It would be done, finished, over. If there was a problem in that part of the United States, then the judge could be the culprit that handed down the verdict. Or James could wire his best friend a note and tell him to go to the nearest lawyer and ask about a divorce. They had spent the night together in the same house after the shotgun vows were said. That could constitute consummation of the marriage. Their word *might* hold up in court; but then again, a judge might tell them they had to file a divorce instead of an annulment.

James ground the cigar out in a crystal ash tray. He chose the right papers from his file cabinet and filled in all the necessary blanks. If Everett wanted an annulment, James Beauchamp would fight for one. He blew on the ink to dry it faster and folded it neatly before he slipped it into an envelope. He put on his hat and coat and started out of the office when the feeling down deep in his soul made him turn right back around. He plopped down behind his desk and propped his feet up, without taking off his hat.

"Good morning, Mr. Beauchamp," his secretary, Molly, said from the outer office. "Coffee?"

"No thank you, Molly," he said, tearing the envelope and its contents into shreds.

"Did you hear about Carolina Prescott?"

"You mean Everett Dulanis's fiancée?" he asked, the feeling becoming stronger and stronger.

"Used to be. She and her father went up there to

Oklahoma where he relocated. My cousin works at the plantation as a seamstress. She helped work on a new wardrobe for Carolina. She went to Oklahoma to break it off with Mr. Dulanis. She's in love with another man. Some fellow Mr. Dulanis went to college with. I think his name is Gatlin but I didn't catch the last name. Anyway, instead of making a wedding dress like my cousin was originally hired to do, she made several new outfits. Carolina was all swoony, just couldn't wait to travel to Philadelphia so she and Gatlin could announce their engagement. I guess Mr. Prescott is deeding his aunt's house over to Carolina and Gatlin. That big one south of town. This Gatlin fellow is going to set up a doctoring office in the parlor," Molly said.

"Well, do tell, *cher,*" James said brightly. "So we find out that the lovely Carolina does not love my friend as much as she said she did."

"Hummmph," Molly said, pushing back her graying hair. "Carolina Prescott won't ever love anyone half as much as she does herself."

The idea was born in the twinkling of a Cajun's eyes as James digested all he'd heard and added it up with the words on the telegram lying on his desk. "Molly, I'm going to be gone for several days. There is nothing pressing on my calendar for the next two weeks. You know how slow this time of year always is. How would you like a few days off?"

"I would love it," Molly said, grinning. "Got grandchildren coming home for Thanksgiving and it would be nice to spend time with them."

"Then we shall take the month of November off . . . with pay. You spend some time with your family, and I shall do a bit of traveling," James said. The feeling settled down. He'd made the right decision at last. Is this the way it worked? When he got the right thing sorted out in his mind, it brought about peace? He didn't know. But there just seemed to be one thing to do: that was, go to where the problem was and study it before the matter went before the judge.

Carolina was a picture of grace and beauty as she appeared at the top of the curving staircase. Her dress was pure white bridal satin designed in the newest fashion, showing off her tiny waist. A soft lace veil covered her face but Everett would know his sweet love anywhere. She literally floated down the stairs on her father's arm. When they reached his side, the preacher asked who gave the woman in marriage.

Mr. Prescott smiled at Everett, his eyes twinkling. "Her mother and I do," he said, loud and clear. He placed the bride's hand in Everett's and joined Mrs. Prescott, who dabbed her eyes with a dainty handkerchief.

The preacher began the standard ceremony. Everett could scarcely believe his good luck in Carolina coming to her senses at the last minute. When she'd written him a soul-searching letter dotted with her own tears. She loved him. She would move to Oklahoma. When the preacher said Everett could kiss the bride, he raised the veil, only it wasn't Carolina that he'd vowed to love for all eternity. Maggie smiled up from under the veil and raised her lips for the kiss to seal their love for all eternity.

Everett sat up in bed, drenched in sweat. The dream had been so real. Right up until he lifted the veil and there was Maggie with her impish grin. He mopped the sweat from his brow with the shirt he'd tossed on the chair beside his bed. Before he could fall back on the bed, a heavy knock came to the door. He jerked on his trousers and was down the ladder when the knock came again, this time louder and longer.

"Hold on," he called out at the same time Maggie opened the door to her bedroom.

"Doc, you in there?" a man's voice yelled.

Maggie reached the door before he did. "Ike, what's the matter? Is it Ruby's time?" she asked.

"Yes, and something ain't right. She's in awful pain this time," Ike said, his face white with fear.

"I'm putting my shoes on and it'll take me five minutes to get the buggy ready. Can you lead the way?" Everett asked.

"You go on back to Ruby, Ike. Five minutes is a long time when you're a hurtin'." Maggie shoved him toward his horse. "I'll come with Everett and show him the way. Tell Ruby we'll be there ten minutes behind you," she shouted as Ike left.

Everett set his jaw and clenched his fists. "You're not going with me, Maggie. I don't need you."

"I guess you do." She shut the door to her bedroom with a loud bang. "Less you figure you know the way to Ike's place," she yelled through the door as she jerked the night rail over her head and grabbed the green dress she'd worn the day before from the back of a chair. Drat all those little buttons down the front. She'd make herself a dress later in the week with only four buttons down the front to throw on when there was a medical emergency she needed to help Everett with. What was she thinking of? By the end of the week she'd be in Guthrie, maybe even Enid if she couldn't find some kind of work in Guthrie.

"You are not going! I'll get the buggy ready and you can give me directions," he yelled back through the door. All he needed was another person to worry with during a difficult birthing. Even though Maggie had proved her mettle earlier in the week with little Alford, it wasn't the same thing as watching the birth of a baby, especially if it was breech, or feet first.

She was waiting on the porch for him. Two loaves of bread, a pint of plum jelly, and two quarts of soup inside a basket at her feet. If he thought she was staying home then he was a fool as well as dull and club-footed when it came to dancing. She heard the horse snorting before the buggy rounded the end of the house.

"Okay, which way is it?" he asked.

She picked up her basket and crawled up beside him on the buggy seat. "Start off toward town. I'll show you as we go."

"I said you aren't going," he said.

"I'm going. Now you going to drive or argue?" she asked.

"Argue, if that's what you want. Your friend is lying there in labor hurting. Just remember that while we're sitting here fighting, Maggie," he said.

"You can't make me feel guilty either, Everett. I'm going. I was there when she had the first two little boys. Momma's been delivering babies longer than you have, and I've been helping her for years. I'm going and that's a fact," she said.

"That doesn't matter. I said you aren't going, and you aren't. I don't need any help. I'm a doctor, not a midwife." He folded his arms across his chest and waited.

Maggie lowered her chin and looked him right in the eye by the light of the full moon. "If she dies, Ike won't be gunnin' for me but for you," she finally said. "You are the doctor."

"Oh, have it your way. But you better stay out of my way," he said, flipping the reins and setting the horse off at a trot. What else was there to learn about Maggie? Everyone said she was slow-witted, yet every time he turned around she amazed him even more. How could she learn so much in, what? Eighteen years? Good grief, she was just a child compared to his almost thirty years. At least Carolina had been twenty, and even that seemed like a big age gap.

"How old are you, Maggie?"

"That's a rude question to ask a lady. Ha—that's funny, ain't it, Everett. You sure don't think you got a lady for a wife. So what matter does it make? I'm twenty-four years old." Maggie chuckled into the dark.

"Why haven't you married?"

"I did. I married you," she reminded him.

"But before?"

"I said I wouldn't marry a man who couldn't dance or who didn't make me laugh. Life is tough. Ain't many of us got the kind of money you grew up with, Everett. I knew I'd have a hard row to hoe when I married. I don't mind hard work. I've done more than my share of it all my life. But if I've got to work then there should be some joy in it. A Saturday night barn dance in the summer months. A good hearty laugh at the end of a day. Without it, I'd grow to resent the fellow I was hitched up with. It's not so much to ask, and it's all I want. There was those who come along who could dance all right. But they were stiffer and primmer than a school marm on Sunday morning. Then there was some who could make me laugh but they had two left feet," she said.

Everett tried to take in everything she'd said. It really wasn't so much for Maggie to reach out toward. Whoever said she was dumb surely didn't know her very well. "And just how many years have you been helping your mother?"

"Since I was fifteen. She didn't want me to see such a thing, being so young and all, but she had to have some help. Elenor was thirteen and Grace eleven. There's two years between all of us. Elenor is now twenty-two and Grace will be twenty in a couple of weeks. Anyway, back then, Momma called on me to help. Nearest doctor was probably a hundred miles away, so that was out of the question. Baby was too big to be born, and she told me what to do and I did it." Maggie's voice caught and she turned her head to hide the tears.

"What happened?" he asked.

"My sister was seventeen. She'd just got married the year before. A big old strapping boy of nineteen. They had a little farm next to ours. His name was Daniel. He died of the cholera when they'd been married six months. She come back home to live with us and have her baby. Only the little boy was too big. They died about ten minutes apart. Momma said she just didn't have the energy to live after two days of hard labor." When Maggie shut her eyes she could see the beautiful little baby laid in her sister's arms when they put her in the wooden casket and buried her.

"I'm so sorry," Everett whispered.

"Millicent was her name." Maggie kept talking. "We called her Milly. She was the pretty one—all this pretty blonde hair, and smart. Oh, my, but she was so smart, Everett. I was two years younger and the dumb one. Always saying the wrong things at the wrong times. Momma told Daddy later that night that it should have been me who died. It was almighty hard on Momma to lose Milly. She looked just like Momma did when she was a young girl, and Momma just fairly well doted on her. I might die like that someday, but I want to laugh and live first."

"Your mother was just grieving, Maggie. People say things like that when they're hurting. I'm sure she didn't mean it," Everett said.

"Could be. I never let on that I heard her say that to Daddy. They was both pretty torn up over it. Never seemed to get past losing her until we heard about the land run, and that put some spark back in them. Turn right down that lane." She pointed down a path that was little more than two wagon wheel ruts with grass grown up between. "See the lights down the way. That dug-out house. Ike's been working on getting a cabin up for the family, but he had to get the crops in first. Ruby hoped they'd have it build before the baby come. Just didn't work that way."

Ike met them at the door and motioned for them to come inside. Two little boys, aged two and one, huddled on a cot in the corner of the one-room, dirt-floored dugout. Their mother lay in the middle of the bed, trying hard not to make noises that would frighten them. A pot of water boiled on the woodstove which had been vented out one of the windows. At least Ike had the foresight to get that ready.

"Okay, let's see what we've got here." Everett tried to speak soothing words as he touched the woman's stomach and lifted the sheet.

"Hey guys, let's me and you go outside and make a pallet under the stars." Maggie gathered up a couple of blankets from a box in the corner. "Now, Robert, you can walk like a big boy and I'll carry Raymond. If you need me Everett, you just call out. We won't go so far that I can't hear your voice. These boys will be back asleep in half an hour."

Everett nodded. "I'm going to do an examination now, Ruby. I'll try to keep it from being painful."

The woman grasped the edge of the sheet, her fingers turning white as she fought to keep from crying out. Neither of her boys had brought her this kind of misery. Like her Aunty said, there was long labor and there was short labor but there wasn't no such thing as easy labor. Well, what she'd had with them was as easy as baking an apple pie compared to this wrenching pain.

"You've done most of the hard work," Everett said. "What we've got here is a breech birth. I'm going to try to turn this baby around so he can make some progress."

"She," Ruby said through gritted teeth.

"Well, that explains it," Everett said. "A girl would give her mother a problem like this."

Maggie slipped back into the room. "The boys are sleeping in a bed I made from dried leaves. Can I help?"

"Tell him it's a girl," Ruby moaned.

Maggie dipped up a basin of cold water and dipped a cloth in it. "Of course it's a girl. It's time for a girl. Two boys are enough to gray a mother's hair." She wiped the sweat from Ruby's face.

"Push, Ruby," Everett said. "Push hard. That's good. One more time. She's got black hair."

Ruby squinted her eyes shut and pushed. The pain was enough to give her a vision of the Pearly Gates, but that horrible, excruciating ache had subsided. This was normal pain. Thank goodness, Dr. Everett knew what to do.

"One more time," Everett said. "That's good. One more. Well, guess what? We've got a baby girl."

Tears flowed down Maggie's cheeks when Ruby opened

her eyes and smiled. She wasn't going to die. Not like Milly had. Every time Maggie went with her mother, she lived in fear that the mother wouldn't open her eyes.

The baby let out a lusty, loud cry and Ike grinned. "She's a beauty, Ruby. Going to look just like you."

Everett laid the baby in Ruby's arms. Maggie tossed the water in the basin out the door, refilled it with warm water and picked up a clean rag. "Let me clean her up for you, Ruby. Won't take but a minute. I'll have her ready for breakfast before Dr. Everett gets his job finished. I brought fresh bread for your breakfast. Ike, you make the boys some oatmeal and slice one loaf for breakfast. There's soup for your dinner meal and another loaf of bread. By supper word will be out you had the baby and there'll be someone bringing in food the next several days." Maggie talked as she worked with the newborn baby. She'd bathed lots of them in the past six years, but this one was exceptionally pretty. Lots of dark hair and plump little wrinkles on her upper thighs and arms.

"Thanks, Maggie," Ruby said, shutting her weary eyes.

"All finished," Everett said.

"Then we'll get her bedding changed," Maggie said. "Here, Ike, you hold this baby while we take care of that." She handed a bright-eyed little girl dressed in a diaper and a long white gown, and wrapped snuggly in a white blanket, to her father.

"Did you find the gowns?" Ruby muttered.

"I knew right where everything was. Remember I was here before," Maggie said.

Everett had never had an assistant so adept at helping him change a bed. Everything about the dumb Maggie continued to amaze him. From the way she could cook, iron his shirts to perfection, sew her own dresses, hold down a rambunctious toddler for stitches, and help deliver a baby. How could anyone ever tag her as anything less than super intelligent? It amazed him.

"I think you're ready to let her have her first meal now," Maggie said. "That is if the proud papa will give her up."

Relaxed. That's the gift Maggie brought to every situation. Peace and a sense of relaxation. Except when she was angry. Then it was bar the door and hide under the bed, because she wouldn't take no for an answer. A strange combination of determination and control in a woman. One that Everett had never encountered before.

Maggie's eyes drooped. She wanted to sleep so badly but that would mean leaning over on Everett's shoulder, and she wouldn't do that if a whole band of Irish leprechauns promised her half the gold in the world. When they got back to the main road, he'd asked directions and she'd told him which way to turn to get home.

"Hey, I recognize this place now that it's the light of day," he said. "We are about half way between the cabin and Guthrie."

"That's right," she'd said with a yawn.

"Well, then we'll go to Guthrie first and see if James has sent me a telegram saying the papers are on the way. It'll keep me from having to drive all the way there later today," he said.

Had Maggie had her gun, she would have shot him right between his pretty brown eyes. She was tired, had breakfast to prepare, and today was the day she made bread. She'd taken the last two loaves in the house to Ruby. He whistled while he drove. She nodded. Her head bouncing around like a ball in a rain barrel.

"Must you whistle?" she snapped.

"Bringing healthy babies into the world makes me happy," he said right back with an edge to his voice. *Women!* They'd never understand the joys of being a doctor.

"Why must they always be born at night?" she wondered aloud, rubbing her eyes to keep them open.

Everett just laughed and began another tune. For someone who couldn't dance, he sure could whistle beautifully. She glanced at him from the corner of her eye. He really was quite handsome with all that dark hair and brown eyes. Built right nice, too. Muscles in all the right places. Carolina was an absolute fool to throw him over.

They reached the telegraph office just as the man opened the doors. Everett bounded out of the buggy and grabbed up a sheet of paper. A smile covered his face. So the papers were on the way. In a few days she'd be a free woman again.

He hopped back into the buggy and unfolded the paper. The whistling stopped.

"Well, what does it say?" she asked, sleepy and irritated both.

"James says he's coming to Oklahoma to discuss it with me. There's a hitch because we've slept in the same house since we said our vows. Possibly we'll have to have a full-fledged divorce. He'll be here on Saturday." Everett's voice sounded even more tired than Maggie felt.

It didn't matter to her when the papers came, or even if they came. She could disappear and tell everyone she was a widow. No one needed to know she was a divorced woman who'd never been in any man's bed. She just wanted to go home and take a nap while the bread raised.

Everett picked up the reins and turned the buggy. A divorce. That could take months. Even he knew there had to be grounds for a divorce. And "I don't love this woman and never will," were scarcely what a judge wanted to hear.

"We don't have room for James in our cabin," she said when they were almost home. "I'll ask Violet and Orrin if he might stay there. They've got more room than they know what to do with."

"James can stay in a hotel in Guthrie," Everett said testily.

"He is your friend. You told me he was your lawyer friend and he could undo this. We ain't wealthy folks from the south, Everett, but we're sociable. He can stay at Violet's and you two can have a visit. Think he'll still be here at Thanksgiving?"

"Lord, I hope not. This whole mess better be resolved by then or I'll lose my sanity," Everett said.

Chapter Six

James sat behind a massive oak desk in Orrin Wilde's study. Two big overstuffed royal blue chairs were drawn up in front of the desk, waiting for Maggie and Everett to arrive. A fire was laid in the stone fireplace on the far wall. It wouldn't be too many more weeks until the mornings would be brisk enough to warrant starting that fire. James wished he could be there when it came that time. He liked what he'd seen of the Indian Territory so far. The area was a bit backward, but it was still in the birthing stages. In twenty years it would be a real state, James was sure. A good lawyer who had a little foresight could set up a practice in this beautiful open country. He could dig his heels in tightly and still be only fifty years old even if it did take twenty years. He'd be in a position to run for a government office and just the right age to do so. Old enough to be established. Young enough to still have the spit and vigor to fight for a new state.

He toyed with a piece of paper while he waited. He'd checked with the judge the day before; there would have to be a divorce. Everett wasn't going to like it one bit, but James wasn't going to argue with the judge. He could have, since the judge wasn't so adamant about the issue. He might have won favor over a deck of cards, because he'd found out when he did his homework that the old fellow did enjoy a good game of poker. But that silly gut feeling kept haunting him.

"Hello," Maggie said when she and Everett opened the door from the foyer. "How are you today? Finding everything all right here at Violet and Orrin's?"

"Never had it better." James smiled and stood up to greet them. Everett never had been blind before, but he had grown scales over his eyes since coming to the territory. Maggie was a breath of fresh air after the prim and proper ladies in Atlanta. She was outspoken; kind to a fault; so naturally beautiful it just plain took James's breath away. His poor friend Everett had to be sightless to miss all that. The best thing was that Maggie was in love with Everett. She didn't know it yet but James did. When a woman looked at him like she did Everett, he fully well intended to hog tie her and carry her to the nearest courthouse for a wedding.

"I'm glad," Maggie said. "I'm just sorry we don't have more room at the cabin. You will be much more comfortable here. Violet said both dogs already took up with you."

"Good hounds. That Missy is a hunter for sure. Don't know about Katy. She's a pet dog, I'm thinkin', *cher,*" James said.

"What does that mean? *Cher.*" Maggie cocked her head to one side and looked at him through the most gorgeous green eyes ever.

Her complexion was opposite to that of any redhead he'd ever seen. Most of them had freckles. Not Maggie. Her skin was a mixture of fresh Georgia peaches mixed with pure cream. To say her hair was red was actually doing it an injustice. It was more like the burgundy leaves on a black maple in the fall of the year. A rich, deep scarlet like none other he'd known.

"It means something like honey, or darling, in Cajun," Everett translated for her.

"Oh." Maggie blushed.

"I did not mean to embarrass you, *ma jolie fille.*" James's voice was silky smooth.

He wasn't as tall or as good looking as Everett but he'd still turn lots of heads on Sunday morning when they went to church, Maggie figured. Dark thick eyebrows rested at the top of eyes so dark brown, at first they appeared to be black as a cloudless midnight sky. He combed his wavy black hair straight back, just like Everett did.

"And what does that mean?" Maggie asked.

"It means *my pretty girl,*" Everett said, fast growing tired of the game. "*C'est assez,* my friend. We came to see what you found out from the judge."

James smiled brightly. "That means it is enough, Maggie, *cher.* Time for business, I suppose. I found out that you will have to file for a divorce. It does not have to be filed in the same county in which you were married or granted in the same state. I will file for it in the state of Georgia where I know more people since you evidently do not have grounds for a divorce."

"Yes we do," Maggie said defiantly. "The grounds are that neither of us want to be married to the other one. If my daddy hadn't forced us with a shotgun we wouldn't be married, so that's grounds for a divorce. Forced."

"I don't think so." James chuckled.

"Then get it started when you go home. I always spend Christmas with Eulalie, so I will sign the papers at that time. I suppose I could bring them back here for Maggie to sign?" Everett asked.

"We'll see how things are progressing then," James said. "Tell me, are you absolutely sure that you could never work this marriage out? Maggie seems a good enough woman to me, my friend. Matter of face, I'd say she's a *'tite ange* from what I've seen this week. She can cook like a gourmet. She works her fingers to the bone, and she's right easy on the eyes."

"That's a little angel." Everett's heart began to stir in his chest. James was goading him with all the Cajun endearments. Trying to make him jealous of his own wife. Well, she wouldn't be his wife for long. She didn't want to be married to him any more than he wanted her for a wife. Sure, she did all the things she was supposed to do and did them well, and she wasn't hard on the eyes. But Maggie didn't love him. She wanted someone to make her laugh and who could do those silly countrified dances. When and if Everett ever did fall in love with a woman again, she was going to take him just like he stood. A serious doctor who liked his life organized and proper.

"Thank you," Maggie said. "But Dr. Everett does not want to be married to me. I could never be the kind of wife he wants or needs, James. I'm just what you see. A country girl."

"Oh, Maggie," a soft voice called from the foyer. "Maggie, Violet said I'd find you inside. Hello?"

"Elenor!" Maggie jumped up.

"Hello?" Elenor said a little louder.

"In here." Maggie opened the double doors into the study. Her eyes were bright when she saw her sister's open arms and she met her in the hallway in a fierce hug.

"I'm so sorry for all those mean things I said about you when I brought your things to you. It was hateful and ugly of me and I should be whipped. If you never speak to me again, I'll understand. It's what I deserve. But I've just missed you so much. I don't care what Daddy says, I'm coming to see you. Don't matter to me how you got married or what happens. I miss my big sister," Elenor said as she hugged Maggie.

Maggie inhaled deeply, love oozing out of her heart. She'd missed Elenor, too. She'd missed the late night gossip sessions after a hard day's work. She'd missed fixing Elenor's long blonde hair for church on Sundays; missed sewing dresses with her sister. Elenor did the machine work most of the time and left the fancy hand work for Maggie, since she had a better hand for it.

"I missed you, too," she said. "It's forgiven. We won't

talk about it no more. I'm glad you've come for a visit. Come inside and meet James. He's Everett's friend from Georgia. A lawyer."

"Why is he here?" Elenor tried to find something in Maggie's eyes to tell her everything was all right, but there was a veil over those deep green eyes that hadn't been there before. Was Everett going to put Maggie aside after all? She'd be ruined for life? If that was the case then Elenor might borrow her father's gun and shoot him graveyard dead. Better that Maggie be a widow than a divorced woman. Widows at least garnered a little respect. Divorcees were lower than the barmaids in the tavern over in Guthrie.

"He's just come for a visit," Maggie lied. "Come and meet him. He's staying through the Thanksgiving holiday. Oh, I'm so glad you've come, Elenor. Is Momma still mad at me? I have a thousand questions to ask!"

"Momma is coming around," Elenor said, then stopped in her tracks. The man behind the desk was the most beautiful creature she'd ever seen in her life. Dark hair, twinkling dark eyes, and a smile that lit up the whole room. A nervous twitch began low in her stomach and warmed her insides. She wished she'd worn her Sunday frock instead of her plain old yellow calico. Her hair was a fright she was sure, and oh, my, there was a bit of mud on the toe of her shoe.

"James, I want you to meet my sister, Elenor," Maggie said with a smile.

James was on his feet before he looked up but when he did his knees went to jelly. An angel had just dropped out of Heaven and stood beside Maggie. If he thought Maggie was breathtaking with all that strange-colored red hair, then her sister was simply gorgeous. He had never believed in love at first sight . . . not until that moment.

Everett turned to see just what had made his friend's face light up like it did the first time they'd actually seen a barmaid on the streets in Terrebonne County. Elenor? Was he besotted with one of the Listen girls? James, who had outrun every woman in Louisiana and Georgia? Surely not!

Maggie kept waiting for someone to say something.

"Did I interrupt something important? I could come back later," Elenor finally said. *Her voice is like fine honey mixed with just a drop of pure white lightning. I could listen to that voice for the rest of my life,* James thought. "Oh, no, *ma jolie fille,* you have arrived at just the right time. We have finished our bit of business. I'm most glad to meet you, Miss Elenor. It is Miss, isn't it?"

"Yes, it is," Elenor drew her brilliant sky blue eyes down in a frown.

"What he just said means my pretty girl," Maggie said with a laugh.

"Yes, it does." James crossed the room, feeling like he was floating. "And I've never seen a more beautiful *cher,* either. Now, I have not seen nearly all of this lovely farm of Orrin and Violet's. Please take this poor southern Georgia cracker for a tour of this area while Everett and Maggie finish their discussion. I would be glad to return you in half an hour, no more, to your sister. But she has you always and I've only just met you. So?"

Elenor could no more have refused James Beauchamp than she could have sprouted the wings of an eagle and flown to the moon. She slipped her arm though his, amazed at the jolt traveling through his jacket sleeve to her fingertips. Wasn't that just the luck? She'd fallen in love at first sight with a lawyer. A fine southern lawyer who would never even consider a simple Oklahoma girl like her.

Maggie sat down in the chair beside Everett and waited until the door slammed. "Good grief, I believe they were both thunderstruck."

"Thunderstruck?" Everett asked.

"You know, thunderstruck. Kind of like the bolt of lightning jumped out of the sky and hit them both and then the thunder hit and they knew they were already in love," Maggie said. "I've heard of it all my life but thought it was just an old wives' tale."

"Well, if I hadn't seen it with my own two eyes I would have never believed it," Everett said. "But James will get over it, I'm sure."

"Why should he?" Maggie asked. "Elenor is of age now. Twenty-two to be exact. And she's a pretty woman. She can cook and sew and . . . are you saying my sister isn't good enough for your friend?"

"I'm saying that they come from two different worlds. She'd be as miserable in his proper world as he would be in hers. That's what I meant. That they are physically attracted is evident, but it takes more than that to build a marriage. Why are we having this conversation anyway?" Everett said, throwing up his hands in exasperation. Trying to explain something so intense as life to Maggie was like expecting her to become a lady overnight.

"I think we are talking about me and you, not them," Maggie said bluntly. "You see your friend in the same predicament you are in."

"I do not." Everett felt high color filling his cheeks as he lied.

"Yes, you do. Well, it don't have to be that way Everett Jackson Dulanis. Not with them, it don't. If they want to fall in love, that's their business, and none of yours. My sister will make anyone a proud wife. All she asks is the same thing I want: a man to love her for just what she is. But you wouldn't understand that," Maggie said.

"And what's that supposed to mean?" Everett jumped out of his chair and stomped over to the window to watch James and Elenor strolling over the rolling hills behind the house. Someday Violet would have flower gardens out there but the house was so new, it simply sat in the middle of the wilderness in which it had been built. James strutted like he was taking the governor's daughter through the gardens at Crooked Oaks. Even in the distance, Everett could see Elenor look up at him in awe.

"If you don't know, I'll be danged if I tell you," Maggie said. "I'm going out on the porch and wait for her to come back. She missed me. She said she did."

"Don't use such crass language. It isn't becoming," Everett said without turning around.

"Drop dead, Everett Dulanis. I'll say what I want, when I want. It don't matter anyway. Because by Christmas I'll be a divorced woman, and they're wild and say anything they please. I imagine I can find a job over in Guthrie at the saloon. Goodness only knows no one in this area is going to hire me to work for them once I'm divorced," she said. "No woman would want me in her house. I might take her husband away from her. No one will want me to keep their children. I could put bad ideas in their heads."

"You can go away and tell people that you are widowed," he said, emotionless.

"That's a lie. Might as well just go to hell for being a divorced woman as for lying," she said. "You just leave James and Elenor alone. If they find they love each other after all, you keep your mouth shut. I mean it."

"Or what?" he practically growled.

"They might not even like each other," Maggie said. "But if they do, you're going to let it alone. Let nature have its way. Don't you step in and make trouble."

"Or what?" he repeated.

Maggie bit the inside of her lip. "I want my sister to be happy. I don't care if she marries up with Ivan Svenson over on the next farm to ours or that fancy lawyer friend of yours. It don't matter one bit to me. But if that lawyer makes her happy and makes her eyes light up like Emma's does when Jed walks in the door, or like Violet's does when Orrin is standing next to her, then she'll have the lawyer. And if you make trouble for her, then Everett Dulanis I will refuse to sign the papers."

"You wouldn't dare." Everett wanted to shake her until her there wasn't a red hair left on her head. Until her teeth rattled and those mesmerizing green eyes popped right out of her skull.

"I would. I don't want to be married to you but I'll stay married to you if you make trouble for Elenor. If they don't like each other, that's fine, but if they do, you'll stay out of it or you'll stay married to me for all eternity. So, that's what. I might be dumb and a hog in a wallow when it comes to being a proper wife to you, but I'm speakin' my mind right now. That's the way it's going to be."

Everett clenched his fists to his side. Surely James wouldn't fall for a country girl like Elenor. This was a simple flirtation. But he wasn't going to back down from a fight with a simple-minded woman like Maggie either. She wasn't going to tell him what he could and couldn't do. Not even if she was downright beautiful when she was angry. All that red hair twisted up on top of her head. Those green eyes dancing in determined rage. And the set of her small shoulders, drawn up in defiance. Even after the way her family had thrown her out, after the hurting words Elenor had said when she brought Maggie's things that day, Maggie still loved them.

"So?" she said, barely above a whisper.

"I won't see my friend make a mistake as big as the one I made," Everett said, a bit cockier than he'd planned.

"Oh? Well, then, you can stay married. I'll tell the judge that I don't want a divorce and that I love you with my whole heart," Maggie threatened.

"That's a lie and you could go to hell for it." Everett turned her earlier words back on her.

"So, seems like I'm doomed for misery in this life and the one to come no matter what. Elenor, on the other hand, might have some happiness," Maggie said.

"Hey, you two, where are you?" Violet called from the foyer. She carried a basket filled with wild flowers over her arm. "Next year I'll have fall flowers. Zinnias, mums, and maybe a few fall roses. Did you see Elenor and James? Lord, I think they've both been thunderstruck."

Everett rolled his eyes and walked out of the room. "Thank you again for keeping James," he said formally as he passed Violet. "I'm going to my office. Ruby is bringing her new baby in this afternoon for a checkup."

"Whew," Violet whistled through her teeth when he shut the front door. "You two fighting?"

"Always," Maggie said.

Violet threw back her head and laughed so hard she had to wipe tears from her cheeks. "That's the best news I've had in weeks."

"Why? Fighting isn't the way married people act," Maggie said, bewildered. "Besides, we aren't really married and you know it. He sleeps in the loft. I sleep behind a closed door in my bedroom. We just share a house. And now James says we can't get an annulment. We have to get a divorce. You know what that's going to do to me, Violet?"

Violet nodded, trying to keep serious since Maggie was on the verge of tears. But she'd bet her new Sunday bonnet that they never did get around to signing those papers. "It will be all right, Maggie. You can stay with me and help take care of my new baby if that time comes. I'll need a housekeeper and someone to help. Orrin's been after me to hire someone already. We'll build you a little house out back and to the devil with what the people say about you. Me and you will know better. Just like we did when Orrin lived with me all that time. You stood beside me and didn't let the gossip bother you none. Now what are you two fighting about?"

"Thank you, Violet." Maggie brushed away a tear. At least her future was secure; and right here in Dodsworth where she was at home. She could see Elenor, even if the rest of her family disowned her. "He thinks Elenor isn't good enough for James. We had words because of that."

"But they just met," Violet said.

"Yes, but they were both thunderstruck, and you know what that could mean. I ain't having Everett interfere if it is love."

"I see," Violet said. "Were you two fighting over that or was it just the kindling for the fight of whether you two might actually fall in love?"

"Wouldn't do me no good to fall in love with him. He said I'd fit his bill for a wife about like a sow in a wallow," Maggie said miserably.

"He's a horse's rear end for talking to you like that," Violet said.

"No, don't call him that. He's a good man and he's right, you know. He's a doctor for goodness sake, Violet. He needs a proper wife who can help him. He don't need someone like me. I'm just a simple country woman. I should have chased Ivan Svenson and been married months ago. At least we would've been on the same level," she said.

Violet just shook her head. Maggie Listen Dulanis was falling in love with her husband and didn't even know it. But she would in time. And divorces took lots of time.

"So what did he say when you told him to stay out of their business?" Violet asked.

"It wasn't what he said but what I said that was mean. I told him that if he interfered with my sister, I wouldn't sign the papers," Maggie said. "I would though. I wouldn't shackle him to me but I want him to think I wouldn't because if that lawyer out there is meant for Elenor, I mean for her to have him. Here they come. Please don't say nothing. I wouldn't hurt her feelings for anything. And like you say, might be it was just us seeing things that wasn't there anyway."

"I wouldn't think of it," Violet smiled sweetly.

Chapter Seven

Maggie dressed carefully in a long-sleeved olive green dress she'd made the previous fall. The waistline was a little big, but then, she hadn't had much of an appetite lately. She twisted her hair up, secured it with several hair pins, and checked her reflection in the mirror above the wash stand in the bedroom she'd been using for several weeks now. Dark circles under her eyes attested to the fact that she hadn't been sleeping well. Four more weeks and she'd be a divorced woman. James planned to go home tomorrow morning and by Christmas he'd have pulled enough strings that the papers would be ready. Everett would sign them when he was in Georgia at his sister's house for Christmas. That would be a good time for her to move to Violet's and to let the word out that she and Everett weren't going to stay married. He'd bring the papers home and, of course, she'd sign them. She wouldn't make someone as intelligent and prominent as Everett stay married to her.

"Well, that's the way it's going to be. Who would have thought I could get myself in this much of a mess just by going to the last dance of the year," she whispered.

"You 'bout ready, Maggie?" Everett called from the living room.

"Almost," she yelled back. She picked up her winter coat. It was faded, but the wool was still good and her mother had helped her re-line it two winters ago. She thought about the gorgeous outfit Carolina had worn when she appeared out of nowhere the day after the shotgun wedding. Did Atlanta ever get blue northers like the one that blew into Oklahoma last night? If so, what kind of coat did Carolina wear? What kind of coat was a real doctor's wife supposed to wear anyway? Somehow, Maggie didn't think it was a faded gray wool with its second or third lining.

Everett warmed his hands by the fireplace and Maggie bit her lip to keep from gasping. Seemed like he just got more handsome every day. Those pretty light brown eyes with yellow flecks in them. All that thick hair always combed back perfectly. His clothes hung on his body like they'd been tailored for his size. Which they probably were, Maggie reminded herself.

"What can I help you carry?" he asked. He didn't need to look up to know she'd entered the room. The aura that preceded her played havoc with his senses. Yes, she was attractive. Yes, she had the sweetest nature of any woman he'd ever been around. Except when she was on her soap box about this thing with James and her sister, Elenor. Good grief, but that was an ugly coat she wore. That dull gray did nothing for her hair or her eyes—yet she was still beautiful even in it. Carolina wouldn't have worn that coat if it had meant she was going to take pneumonia and die the next day. But then Carolina would be celebrating the holidays at her father's plantation, Gatlin beside her at the dinner table. He waited for the pangs of sorrow and pain, but they weren't there.

"If you don't mind, you could take that dish of candied sweet potatoes. They're wrapped in a cozy to keep them warm so you won't need hot pads. I'll carry the blackberry cobbler. Then I'll run back in for the pumpkin pies," she said.

He just nodded.

"Seems a bit much to hitch up a buggy for a half mile trip," Maggie said when everything was secure behind the seat.

"How would we get the food there?" Everett slipped his hands around her waist to hand her up into the buggy. Something made his fingers tingle when his hand brushed past hers. Must be this blasted cold wind. Emma never mentioned blue northers when she had answered his letters about relocating in the territory.

"Guess I forgot about that," Maggie said, her quivering hands tucked underneath the blanket Everett tucked around them both.

The front door exploded when they drove up into the yard at Violet and Orrin's house. Mary, Sarah, Jimmy, and Molly along with the two dogs, Missy and Katy, ran out into the cold to greet the last two Thanksgiving Day guests. Emma and Jed were already in the house. James had driven to the Listen house and brought Elenor back more than an hour ago. Emma and Lalie Joy were watching Violet put the final touches on one of her chocolate layer cakes. Luscious odors of cooking turkey, cornbread dressing, and homemade bread filled the whole house and drifted out onto the porch through the open door.

"You're almost late," Mary chided. "But then Momma says you're still on your honeymoon and probably had other things to do. What would you have to do? Huh, Maggie?"

"Oh, hush," Sarah said with a blush. "Here Dr. Everett, let me carry one of those pies. Yummy, pumpkin! And Maggie makes the second best pumpkin pies in the whole world. Almost as good as John Whitebear's wife makes."

Everett cut his eyes around to see Maggie's expression after that comment. High color filled her cheeks. His own face felt flushed. He surely hoped that everyone in the house thought it was only wind burn. Why would a little girl's innocent comment make him blush anyway? He was a thirty-year-old man, not a school boy.

Thinking of being a school boy again made him think of James, whose voice he heard loud and clear in Orrin's study. James Beauchamp had been a busy man the past three weeks. He'd bought a building in Guthrie where he planned to set up practice. Right next door to an empty lot where he planned to build a modest two-story home. Not like the one Orrin built for Violet with all the pillars and bedrooms. More like Emma and Jed's, he'd said. When it was finished he intended to bend his knee and beg Elenor to marry him. Listening to James declaring how much he loved Elenor grated Everett's nerves. His friend was making the biggest mistake of his life and there wasn't a single thing Everett could do to talk him out of it. He'd tried (at the expense of ruining his own future) but James just moaned about having to leave his sweet Elenor for a few months to get his affairs settled.

"Come on Everett, the menfolks are in the den. We've been talking about going out this afternoon for a little bit of hunting. It's cold enough to butcher hogs so Daddy Jed says that we could shoot more than one buck if we got a good sight on them. He said I could go, too." Jimmy tugged at Everett's hand, pulling him across the foyer and into the room with Orrin, Jed, and James.

"Well, the honeymooners did get around in time to make it to the dinner," Jed said, chuckling. "Join us, Everett. We're glad to see the cold snap so we can butcher. Orrin and I are thinking about a little hunt this afternoon. Tomorrow we're going to butcher a steer over at my place, then the next day, a couple of hogs here at his place."

"And I miss all the fun." James grinned. "I suppose you'll have eaten it all up by the time I return?"

"C'est la vie." Everett finally smiled.

"What la who?" Orrin asked.

"It means *that is life* or *this is life,*" James said, and raised his cup of hot coffee in a salute. "He must be in a good mood to be using Cajun. When he left our motherland of Terrebonne County, Louisiana, he seldom ever spoke the language. Honeymooning is good for you, my friend," James winked.

Sarah appeared at Everett's elbow at the same time he sat down. She put a hot cup of coffee in Everett's hands and escaped back to the kitchen where the women were just beginning to pour victuals into bowls. This was her first year to wear long dresses and put her hair up and Sarah wasn't about to miss a word, not even if she did have to raise her skirt tails and run back across the foyer, through the living room, dining room, and to the back of the house where Emma, Violet, and Maggie, and Elenor were discussing menfolks.

She made it in time to hear Elenor giggle about something James had said to her on the way over to the Wilde place that morning. "And he said Everett spends Christmas with his sister every year. I can't imagine getting to go to Georgia just for Christmas. Violet, we've got to start sewing for her tomorrow. She's got to have new things to go down there to that big old plantation. James says there's parties for the holidays and even Christmas balls. I can't imagine all that. Just think of all the dancing, Maggie. Maybe someday I can go," Elenor said wistfully.

Maggie swallowed hard. She wasn't going to Georgia for the holidays. There was no way Everett would take her, nor no way she'd go. If folks here in her own world thought Maggie Listen was a bit short on the smart end of the stick, then she'd embarrass the doctor all to the devil amongst his own kith and kin.

"I think that's a wonderful idea, Elenor," Violet said. "We've got butchering Friday and Saturday. Sunday is church and then next week we could start sewing. Now, when do I need to start designing a wedding dress, Miss Elenor?"

"Is Elenor getting married to Ivan?" Mary looked up from the pallet on the floor where she'd been playing with Lalie Joy.

"No silly," Sarah sniffed dramatically. "Ivan got away. Now she's going to marry up with James."

Elenor blushed scarlet and giggled at the same time. "He hasn't proposed. Not yet. But I keep hoping he might at least hint at it before he leaves tomorrow. Oh, Maggie, how am I going to live six whole months without him?"

"Seems to me that a few weeks ago you were fussing at me for ruining your chances with Ivan Svenson," Maggie said.

"Ivan never did like me," Elenor said. "I just wanted a husband so bad, I would've chased him down. I love James Beauchamp. There I've admitted it. Just like you love Everett Dulanis. No matter how you got married, it's all over your face every time he walks in a room. I 'spect my own face looks about the same whenever James is around."

"You've got love fever," Maggie said shortly. "We'd better be getting this food carried to the table. Menfolks don't love nothing or no one if they are hungry."

"She's learning. The way to a man's heart is through his stomach," Emma said. "Sarah, you take that bowl of potato salad. Be careful with Violet's bowl now."

The name cards at each place setting made the children giggle as they searched for their own seat. They even helped the adults find theirs. Jimmy dragging Everett and James by the hands and stopping them behind the chairs where their cards were located. Sarah pointing the way for Maggie and Elenor. The whole concept might have been humorous to the children, and wonderful to Elenor and James who were seated side by side. But it was a nightmare from the beginning for Maggie, who would have to sit so close to Everett they'd rub elbows.

Like dancing with Jim Parsons, it would be a job, but Preacher Elgin had just said last Sunday that the good Lord didn't put any more upon a person's back than that which they could haul around all day. Seemed lately He'd been testing Maggie's strength pretty steadily, and sitting that close to Everett for an hour or more might just be the last ounce she could abide.

Everett did his duty in seating his wife, but tried diligently not to touch Maggie. However his hand did brush her shoulder when she gracefully sat down, and that same little tingle he'd felt before traveled from his finger tips all the way to his elbow. He frowned. It wasn't cold in the house, not with the warmth of the kitchen stove warming the house as well as the fireplace in the end of the great dining room. Must be some kind of shock his shoes caused due to the cold weather outside and the warm house.

Maggie folded her hands in her lap and bowed her head, gratefully. Grateful that she could shut her eyes even if she couldn't erase the vision of Everett with a frown on his face, knowing that it must have taxed him greatly to treat her like a lady. Grateful for a few moments to collect herself and will the high color from her cheeks put there from the shock of his touch.

"We'll all join hands now," Orrin said, offering his right hand to his wife and his left one to little Molly Thomas who'd begged to sit beside Orrin.

Maggie and Everett both jumped like they'd been shot through with a solid bolt of lightning. The frown returned to his face and she simply put her hand on the table and bowed her head again. He didn't even want to touch her hand. Maggie would bet dollars to dust that he would have had a smile for Carolina if she'd been sitting right next to him at the Thanksgiving table. Finally, she felt his big hand close over her small one. She'd never felt anything like that touch. Not when the little boys in school tried to take her hand when they walked home together. Not when the older boys tried to lace their fingers through hers. Never. She shut her eyes tightly, trying to will her heart to stop beating so fast.

Everett felt the quiver in Maggie's small hand. She'd probably jerk her hand out of his any moment. She certainly didn't want it to be there, not from the way it was shaking. He was only slightly amazed by the heat chasing up and down his forearm as he held her hand loosely. Strange, he hadn't felt like that since the first time he grabbed a little girl's hand on the way home from school. Even then it didn't produce the heady feeling that he was experiencing as Orrin thanked the Father in Heaven for all the blessings they'd had the previous year.

Everett wished he could say a hearty amen when Orrin finished. He couldn't. A year ago, he was firmly engaged to Carolina, their wedding in the first planning stages. Since then he'd moved to this forsaken country, learned to love it and the people—and hate his wife. Who wouldn't despise a woman he'd been shackled to with a shotgun, though? It was absolutely normal for him to feel the way he did about Maggie. He'd wish her no harm, but Lord, he'd be glad when the divorce was over and finalized. Maybe by next year at this time, he could truly agree with Orrin's holiday blessing.

"Now for just a few minutes to start a new tradition amongst us at this table," Violet said. "While Orrin carves this bird, I want each person to tell one thing they've been blessed with in this past year. We'll start with Molly and go around the table. So Miss Molly, what made you happy this year?"

"Well, I was glad when my Orrin married you so he wouldn't have to take Missy and go far away," Molly said seriously.

"I'm glad I get to go hunting with the men folkses this afternoon," Jimmy said.

"I'm happy that I finally growed up enough to get to wear long dresses and put my hair up," Sarah added.

"I'm glad I don't have to put my hair up and act all hoity-toity like Sarah does," Mary said. "But what Sarah is really thankful for is that John Whitebear is paying attention to her. And I'm glad Maggie and Dr. Everett got married because he used to look lonely."

"Lalie Joy," Emma said. She'd have to keep a closer eye

on Sarah. Was Johnny really paying attention to Sarah? He was a good fellow, but how would Jed feel about that?

"Emma," Jed answered, kissing his wife on the cheek. So Johnny Whitebear was eyeing his niece. How wonderful. He was a fine young man who had his heart set on being a lawyer and helping his people.

"I am thankful for my Granny Beauchamp. She had the sight, as we say in Terrebonne County, Louisiana. She knew when her heart was telling her to take care of something important. I think she gave me just enough of that sight to bring me to the territory. I thought it was to help my friend with some legal matters, but it turns out it was to help myself," James said without taking his dark eyes from Elenor's, hoping that she understood what he said even if everyone else in the room only heard riddles.

"Me, I'm just thankful to be sitting at this table with the ones I love the most," Elenor said, speaking volumes to her sister and to James Beauchamp.

Maggie bit the inside of her lip and wrung her hands under the table. She was the newest bride amongst them all and should simply say she was thankful for Everett, but she couldn't embarrass him that way. He'd feel duty bound to say the same thing about her and that would be a blatant lie. She wasn't sure that the ceiling wouldn't open up right over that big turkey and lightning bolts shoot down from the blue skies to strike her graveyard dead.

"Well, Maggie?" Violet prompted her. "Surely you've got something to be thankful for?"

"There's so many things that I'm trying to think of the best one," Maggie said sweetly without looking at Everett. "I guess I'm thankful Daddy didn't have any shells for that shotgun."

Everett's head jerked around to stare at her. "What?"

"Daddy hasn't had shells for that gun in years. He never uses it for real hunting. Something about it messing up the last time his daddy went hunting with it," Maggie said.

"Then he wouldn't have shot me," Everett said incredulously. "And you knew it?"

"I didn't say that." Maggie bowed up to him, her face inches from his, oblivious to all the people around them. The sparks flew between them so fast and furious that the candles strung down the middle of the table paled in comparison.

"Then what did you say? *C'est la guerre!*" Everett demanded. He wouldn't spend another night with her. Not even in the capacity they'd lived together. He'd go back to the cabin and load all her things in the wagon. She could live with Violet until the divorce came through and then she could very well go to the devil as far as he was concerned.

"That means this is war. Me, I think it might be," James translated for her when she looked straight at him. Everett must really be in a snit if he reverted back to the old language again.

"It might be war, Everett, but I said he couldn't shoot you with *that* gun. It's just an old blunderbuss. I didn't say he wouldn't have killed you if you hadn't done just what he said," Maggie said.

"What are you talking about? If the gun wouldn't work, it wouldn't work. Why didn't you tell me then? This could have all been avoided, Maggie Listen," he snapped angrily.

"Maggie Dulanis," Elenor injected smoothly.

"Okay then, Maggie Dulanis," Everett said, his eyes fairly well dancing with rage as he drew out her legal name in an ice cold tone that left no doubt in Maggie's mind she had no right to the name, not even for a little while.

"Are you blind as well as dumb?" Maggie said in exasperation. "Daddy was wearing his pistol around his hips. He could shoot the eyes out of a moving coyote at a hundred yards and not even mess up the hide. The shotgun was there to scare you. The pistol was there for business. If you'd run then you'd a been dead."

"Then why are you thankful that the shotgun didn't have shells. If I was going to be dead anyway?" he asked.

"Because the pistol would have made a little hole in your back and gone through your heart. You might have been dead but it wouldn't have blown your handsome face off. I don't think I could have borne that, Everett Dulanis," she said, using the same tone he'd used when he dragged out the Dulanis in fine southern form.

"Well, hallelujah." James began to clap for the show and to lighten the mood around the table. "Me, neither. If he was going to be dead, I'd rather have seen him with a hole in his stubborn heart, too, instead of his head blown to smithereens. Well done, Maggie, even if it did take a while for you to find something to be thankful for. Now Violet, it's your turn."

"I am thankful for second chances. For Orrin and our life together and for this baby we're going to have in a few months," Violet said sweetly.

"And I'm thankful for the same things Violet is," Orrin piped up from the end of the table.

"We forgot Dr. Everett," Mary said. "Is he thankful the shotgun didn't have shells, too?"

"I am," Everett finally said, and smiled, erasing the stormy look from his face. "And for all my good friends around this holiday table. May we stay friends forever." So she thought he was dumb and he had a handsome face, did she? His silly heart was fluttering around like a school boy's because it would sadden her if his handsome face had been destroyed. His analytical medical mind reminded his heart that she also thought he was dumb. It was nothing short of an oxymoron that couldn't be untangled. "Now, would it be proper to begin to pass these bowls around the table, Violet? As for me and James here, we are starving."

All except me, Maggie thought. *He's thankful for all his friends but that doesn't include me. Because I'm not his friend. I'm not really his wife. I'm not anything to Everett Dulanis and I'm afraid I've fallen in love with the man.*

Chapter Eight

All through the night the snow fell, one feather-light flake upon the other until by morning it was at least ten inches deep. Maggie found Everett sitting before the fire when she opened her bedroom door, just like she did every day. He never said a word to her except an occasional "good morning." Since Thanksgiving dinner the week before, even those two words had ceased. He just couldn't get it through his thick skull that he would have died anyway if he hadn't married up with her that Sunday morning. The shotgun was empty but Ben's pistol wasn't, and his temper was so hot Maggie was surprised blue blazes weren't shooting out the top of his head.

She had made a fire in the cook stove and was on her way to the bedroom to get dressed before she cooked breakfast when she noticed that Patches was still in her box. That was strange. Usually the old girl was up and rubbing all over Maggie's legs, begging to be let outside. When Maggie bent down to rub the cat, her long hair brushed across Everett's arm, tickling the nerve endings but not the heart strings that wound up tighter and tighter every day he had to live with Maggie. She'd made a complete fool of him at the Thanksgiving table, telling everyone she was glad he hadn't had his handsome face blown to bits by her daddy's shotgun. The quicker he could get her out of his cabin and the divorce finalized, the happier he would be.

"Oh!" She gasped and sat down so close to his bare feet that he jerked them back under the rocking chair. "Babies. In the middle of the winter. Don't you know that's not good, you silly old girl," Maggie cooed.

"Babies?" Everett peeked around all that massive red hair to see Patches curled in a semi-circle around a bunch of squirming baby kittens. Well, Maggie could take the whole passel of them to Violet's with her. He hated cats. Barely tolerated Patches, with her shedding hair. Most mornings he had to brush and brush the seat of his trousers to get the white hair off before he went to work.

"Kittens!" Maggie cooed. "Momma cats don't usually have kittens until spring. They'd never live out in the cold. Not even in a barn with lots of hay and mice. But look, Everett, there's three of them. A black one. One like Patches and it's not hard to see who's tom cat she went to visit with this one," Maggie held up a charcoal gray bundle of fur in her hands for him to look at. "Jed's old barn cat is this color. I can't wait to tell the kids about this. They'll all have to come and see, and Molly will be dancing around with joy. She'll probably lay claim to this one."

"She can have all of them," Everett said.

"You don't like baby kittens?" Maggie cocked her head off to one side.

"Baby kittens grow up to be cats. I don't like cats," Everett said.

"Why?" Maggie put the kitten back to his mother's breast where he latched on and began to knead her udder with his small paws.

"Never have," Everett said. "They're okay in the barns where they can kill mice. But house cats are a nuisance."

One more reason for her not to like the man. Anyone who couldn't love a baby kitten wasn't worth her time. "I'm going to get dressed and fix breakfast. Sun sure is taking its slow old time getting up this morning," she said, ignoring his rudeness.

"Ain't coming up," Everett said as she shut the bedroom door; but she didn't hear him. He scooted his chair around so he could see the kittens. Why *did* he hate cats? When he'd been a small child, he'd loved them. Loved the soft way their fur felt against his fingertips. Loved finding a nest of them in the barns at the sugar plantation his father and mother owned. Used to sneak them upstairs into his room and even suffer the wrath of Betsy, the housekeeper, when she found the messes they made. Must have been when he started seeing Carolina and she hated them so much that he decided he couldn't abide them around.

Patches purred contentedly and readjusted her tummy so the black one could find a tit that hadn't been milked dry. Maggie would be a mother like that. Purring. Contented with her family and children. Maybe when it was all over Ivan Svenson would come around to court her. A knot of jealousy twisted his heart up in a wad so tight he could hardly breathe. He wouldn't be jealous. Not of Maggie Listen . . . Dulanis. He wouldn't have ever courted her. He wouldn't have married her except for that empty shotgun. Which was poetic justice. The vows they'd said that day were as hollow as the gun had been.

Maggie slipped out of her flannel night rail and hurriedly dressed in long underwear, drawers, a camisole, and her everyday dress of faded blue checks. She braided her hair and left it hanging down her back, washed her face in the cold water in the wash basin, and stepped into a pair of hand crocheted house slippers. The wood floor was so cold that she figured they were in for a long, hard winter. Maybe it would be too cold and rough for Everett to go to Atlanta the next week. She shook that thought away from her head. They needed to get the divorce over with. As it was, Elenor and Violet were fussing about making new dresses for her to take along to Atlanta. She kept telling them her present wardrobe was good enough for her holiday trip . . . which wouldn't be all that far. Just over to Violet's house to begin her new job as housekeeper and baby-sitter. But she'd decided not to tell them that until the time came.

"Sun really is lazy," she said when she opened the door.

"Isn't coming up today. I told you that already," Everett said, looking up from a thick medical book he had his nose in. Mercy but she was lovely, even in that faded work dress and her homemade slippers. Another time. Another place. Who knows what could have happened between them?

Maggie ignored him and opened the front door. "Snow!" she squealed. "Look, it's deep enough for a snow man and snow ice cream. Can I wear your old trousers again so we can go outside and play after breakfast? You don't think it will melt before then do you? Oh isn't it beautiful. So clean and white—and we're snowed in. You can't possibly go to work in that."

"That's what I said a while ago. You don't listen to anything, do you?" he said irritably. The day he went outside with Maggie to play in the snow is the day they'd have some equally as deep and white in Hades.

Maggie shrugged. Evidently he was hungry and hungry men weren't accountable for their words. Or their actions. "I'll make breakfast and then we'll see. Since you don't have to go to the office, how about some pancakes and eggs?"

"Crepes," he muttered, remembering Granny Beauchamp's delicious crepes when he and James were just boys growing up on adjoining sugar plantations.

"What?" She cocked her head to the side again and Everett wanted to slap her. Not because it irritated him, but quite the rather. It set his senses reeling for her to look at him like that.

"Crepes. Really thin pancakes, browned on both sides, spread with honey whipped in sweet cream butter and rolled up. Served up with soft scrambled eggs and grits on the side," he said.

"Well, I can do the thin pancakes and we got honey and

butter. Eggs are in the basket. But there ain't no grits," she said.

"Isn't any grits," he corrected her.

"That's what I said." She reached for a bowl on the shelf above the dry sink.

Everett just rolled his eyes. One more reason chalked up to common sense over attraction. It would never work even if he wanted it to, which he didn't. He laid the book aside and looked down into the basket where Patches washed the newborn kittens. The gray one hissed and slapped at her, not wanting his face cleaned but rather to be left alone to eat more.

I know just how you feel, old man, Everett smiled. *A hungry man needs his breakfast, not a bath.* He chuckled at the persistence of Patches and the rebel blood in the sightless baby.

"What's so funny?" Maggie couldn't believe that Everett was actually laughing.

"That gray kitten is going to be a handful. I'm laying claim to him before Molly sees them. He's pretty spunky. Come and look at him, Maggie. He's hissing at his own mother and he can't be more than a few hours old." Everett laughed.

Maggie laid her hot pad down and crossed the room, amazement on her face. "I thought you didn't like cats."

"I don't. Hate them. But I like that gray kitten. Look at him swat at his mother's face without letting go of that tit." Everett's eyes danced with merriment.

"Then he's all yours." Maggie giggled at the sight. Patches in all her patience. That little ball of gray fur wanting his way even so early in life. Something tugged at the strings around Maggie's heart. Everett had laughed. Had actually enjoyed something as simple as a kitten. Could there be hope for him?

"He'll keep me company on the long, lonely winter nights. His name is Scrapper." Everett continued to stare at the basket.

The hope died.

Maggie went back to the kitchen, her heart lying like a chunk of sod in August in her heart. Hard, brittle, and aching.

After breakfast she disappeared into the bedroom to don the pants and shirt she'd worn that first Sunday morning they'd gotten married. She was going out to play in the snow, with or without Everett. Maybe Emma and Jed's kids would come down and help her build a snowman. If they were busy erecting their own, then she'd make do by herself. She didn't need Everett Dulanis. Never did. It was just the daily living together that had begun to get under her skin. She peeled off everything but the long underwear and brushed away a tear. She wouldn't let him ruin her whole day with his one ugly remark about a newborn kitten keeping him company on lonely nights. That bit of gray fluff meant more to him than Maggie did. But then, perhaps it should, she thought as she stepped into the pants and buttoned them up the fly. It hadn't been forced on him. He'd picked it out of his own free accord. She grabbed her coat from the hook on the wall and already had it buttoned when she went back out into the living room.

"You really going out in this? It's awfully cold. You might catch pneumonia." Everett looked up from his cozy spot next to the blazing fireplace.

"Wouldn't you be lucky if I did. Save you whatever a divorce would cost," she smarted off as she escaped out the kitchen door into the back yard.

A cold north wind swept across her face and found its way through the wool coat. She pulled a pair of worn gloves from her pockets and shoved her hands down in them. Jed's laughter floated down on the wind along with the children's. Emma's voice joined them in a while, letting Maggie know that they were building their own snowman.

The snow was moist enough to pack together, just right to roll. Maggie started with a ball no bigger than the size of Everett's head. Now where did that thought come from?

She didn't intend to think about that egotistical rascal of a man all morning. He could sit before the fire and watch his new kitten all morning for all she cared. Matter of fact, she just might spend the whole day outside. He could eat left-over crepes for lunch and wash them down with cold coffee.

Everett watched her from the kitchen window. Her face looked almost as dark red as her hair. He searched his repertoire of adjectives, looking for just the right one to describe her strange-colored hair. The closest thing he could come up with was the color of black maple leaves in the fall. But then that wasn't quite right either. It was more like a deep chestnut. That's it. She wasn't a redhead at all, but rather a chestnut brunette.

The coat was still ugly. It had to be the ugliest thing he'd ever seen. If they were really married he would burn the thing and buy her a new one. She looked like a little kid out there playing in the snow, rolling up a huge ball to make the bottom layer for her snowman. Maybe she'd take off her horrid coat and dress the snowman in it when she finished. That would be hoping for too much, Everett thought, shaking his head and going back to his book.

He read three pages and looked down at his new buddy, Scrapper, who was sleeping soundly while his mother proceeded with his bath. A restlessness invaded Everett's soul. He went back to the window. Deep ruts created a maze in the snow where Maggie had rolled the ball around to make the bottom part of her snowman. Her cheeks were even redder. If she didn't have pneumonia by morning, he'd eat his new leather gloves.

He looked at her snow encrusted hands and saw gloves even more disgusting than her wool coat. When he went back into town to his office, he would purchase her a pair of decent gloves at Duncan's store. Maybe two or three pair. One good leather pair for outside; a couple of white lady's gloves for church. She'd fuss and fume and say she didn't want pay for all her hard work, and they'd fight . . . again.

He smiled. That's what they seemed to do best. Fuss and argue. Sometime he'd like to turn her over his knee and give her the spanking she begged for. Sometime he'd like to pick her up and carry her to the bedroom, smothering her pretty face with kisses the whole way, toss her on the bed, and spend the whole afternoon making up like normal honeymooners did.

She had the second enormous snowball ready, and there was no way she was going to lift it alone. Everett sighed. There was nothing to do but go out there and help her and he hated to be cold. That was one of the reasons he left New York. All those long dreary winters.

"You'll never lift that heavy thing alone," he called out as he used the ruts for pathways to keep the wet snow away from his pants' legs.

"I don't need your help," she said. "I can do it by myself."

"No you can't," he argued. "Now, you get on that side and I'll take this one and at the count of three we'll hoist it up on that base you've got built. Grab my hands and it'll make it easier. Lord, girl, why couldn't you be satisfied with a dwarf snowman?"

Because it wouldn't be as tall as you, she thought, but she didn't say a word.

"One." He wrapped his arms around the icy cold ball, his expensive leather gloves covering her worn out work gloves.

"Two." The shock radiating from her hands to his made his heart skip a beat.

"Three." It was just a simple physical attraction born from an abnormal situation. A man and a woman didn't normally live in the same house together unless they were really man and wife.

They both lifted with all their might and almost had the huge ball on top of the other one when it began to slip.

"Hurry," Maggie gasped. "Don't let go. Just a little more. Right there."

"Can we let go?" Everett huffed. He'd never hugged anything or anyone so tightly in his life.

"I think so. Now pack snow around it so it won't roll off," she said, reaching down and picking up as much as she could get in her hand.

"Like this?" he asked.

"Haven't you ever built a snowman?" she asked.

"No, can't say as I have. Grew up in southern Louisiana. Didn't have snow down there hardly ever, and never like this. By the time I saw this much snow I was in New York and despised the stuff," he said, following her lead in packing the white stuff around the snowman's bottom half and its torso.

"Why would you not like something as beautiful as snow?" she asked in amazement.

"It's cold. It's wet. It makes people sick. Sometimes they die and I feel like a failure then," he admitted.

"It's not you that fails," she said. "God just gives us so many days on this earth. When they're done, they're done. You do magic to make those days better for folks, Everett. But when God says it's over, then all the magic in the world can't buy another day. Here, put some right here, and I think we're ready to roll up a little one for his head."

What she said made sense. How could she do that? One minute Maggie was as simple as a child. The next, her wisdom exceeded the sages. "So do you really believe that?"

"What? That we need to make him a head? Well, he'd be pretty sorry looking without one. Maybe we need to make him a wife when we get finished and a bunch of little snow children. We don't get this much snow to work with real often," she said.

"No, one snowman is enough." Everett laughed. A rich, deep laughter that erupted from his chest and made Maggie smile. It was the kind of laugh she wanted to hear every day from the man she eventually married up with. "I meant do you really believe that God says when it's time?"

"Of course I do," she said simply. Everett Dulanis was a complicated man all right, but he wasn't too smart if he doubted the very God of Heaven.

"Okay, let's get a head made for the snowman. I suppose you'll want to put a hat on him and a scarf around his neck, too?"

"Of course," Maggie said, nodding. "And a carrot for a nose and two buttons for his eyes. I've got just the ones saved from when we put new ones on this coat."

They rolled the ball together, side by side. When it was just the right size, they joined hands around it and began to lift it to the top of the snowman. Maggie tiptoed, her feet slipped on a slick patch of ice covered grass, and in less time than it takes a gnat to blink she was on the ground. Moved by the momentum and her hands still tangled up with his, Everett was pulled right down on top of her. The snowman's head banged against the rest of the statue and crumbled all over both of them.

"Whew," Maggie said with a giggle when she could get her breath back. "Guess I slipped."

She looked up into Everett's brown eyes and somehow got lost in them. There was a man hiding behind all that doctoring business who could laugh after all. One who had so much more depth than she'd thought at first. Actually, too much intensity, because right then Maggie was afraid. Frightened of her own feelings. That funny, warm, oozy feeling deep in the pits of her stomach. The way her heart raced. It spelled love. And Maggie didn't want to be in love with Everett Dulanis. It would hurt too bad to lose him if she was in love with him.

Everett's heart matched hers, beat for beat. She was beautiful with the snow frosting her red hair. Those mossy green eyes that were so much a part of her charm locked up with his and something stirred deep inside him. He lowered his head slightly to see even better into the soul of the woman who lay under him. His mouth brushed against her cold lips; then he really kissed her.

It was nothing like the kiss they'd shared the day they married. That one bordered on disgusting. This one warmed the ground beneath them and lit up the gray skies in a palette of artist's colors. Everett tasted the cold morning and sweet honey on her lips and wished the kiss could never end. Maggie tasted the morning coffee on Everett's tongue as it flicked across her lips, making her practically swoon. This was what kisses were meant to be—but not with a doctor who thought she was a country bumpkin. Would anyone else ever stir her heart and soul the way Everett did with one kiss? She doubted it.

"I'm sorry," he said, drawing away and apologizing all at once.

"It's all right." She touched her lips to see if they were as hot as they felt. "I shouldn't have fallen down. Clumsy of me."

"Well then shall we make another head for this snowman?" He cleared his throat but couldn't erase the way he'd felt when he kissed Maggie.

"We'd better. And this time I'll make sure I'm standing on sure footing." She nodded, biting the inside of her lip to make sure she didn't dream that kiss. Apparently it didn't mean as much to him or he wouldn't have apologized.

"Hey, where are you all?" Someone called from the back door and then suddenly every one of the Listens were rushing out to the yard. "We brought the sled over to see you and Momma brought soup for dinner. Hey, you need some help getting that snowman finished. I told Momma you'd be out here playing in it," Grace said.

"Looks like you two had a mishap." Ben grinned. "Here. Let me give you a hand up, son?"

Everett didn't know whether to take the hand in friendship or run for the nearest train leaving Oklahoma. Ben wore the same six-gun on his hip, and the smile on his face could be fake even if he did address him as son.

"Come on, Doc. Let bygones be bygones. We've come to visit, since can't none of us work today. We'll have soup and cornbread for dinner, and maybe these women can come in out of the snow long enough to make us a pie." Ben still held out his hand.

"Momma?" Maggie pushed away from Everett and hugged her mother.

"You are forgiven. Are we?" Her mother, Iris, put her hands on her hips and waited patiently.

"Of course you are, Momma," Maggie grinned.

"Well, that's that. Now you menfolks go in the house and we'll finish playing for a little while," Iris Listen barked orders.

Everett clasped the hand of his father-in-law and Maggie grabbed Elenor's hand. "No, let's all go inside and have some hot chocolate. I made oatmeal cookies yesterday. Guess I knew Daddy might be coming around today, since they're his favorite," Maggie said. "We can finish this snowman later. You've had a long, cold ride over here."

"Guess what?" Elenor blurted out before they'd barely gotten their coats removed and thrown across the rocking chair. "Emma and Jed are going to Louisiana for Christmas, and they've invited me to go with them so I can see James. So I'll be there on Christmas day with you, Maggie. I'm just so excited I could cry."

"But I wasn't planning on going. I changed my mind and decided to stay and help Violet." She searched for words to keep from offending Everett or upsetting her family.

"Posh," Iris said, pouring milk from a gallon jar into a big kettle. "Woman doesn't let her husband go off like that over Christmas without her. I'm surprised Everett don't put you away for talking like that. And you still on your honeymoon. He wouldn't let you stay here for nothing. I bet from the look on his face you hadn't even told him about your thinking either, have you? No, I didn't think so. Why don't you want to go?"

"It's because she wouldn't let me and Violet sew up new things for her, I'm sure," Elenor said. "She sure don't want to go down there amongst all those new people without a few new things, but she's too proud to let me and Violet do for her."

"No, that's not it," Maggie said. Should she tell them right now or wait until the right time after Everett was gone. She looked at the six-gun on her Daddy's hip and remembered his temper. The truce might be the shortest one in all history and she a widow in the next five minutes.

"Well?" Iris said.

"I don't know what Maggie is talking about. Of course she's going with me to Georgia. We'll have a great time, Elenor. James and I will show you girls all around Atlanta. Eulalie wrote last week that there won't be a huge party at the Crooked Oak this year because the babies are so small, and what with Emma and Jed being there with their five. But she is planning a party with a few friends invited. I had thought to surprise you with the idea of going a week early. Eulalie has hired seamstresses to sew that week for the ladies," Everett said and wondered just where all that had come from. He had no intentions of taking Maggie to Georgia, not even if she promised him a dozen more of those tantalizing kisses.

Maggie smiled sweetly. "That sounds like great fun. Now let's get this chocolate ready and thaw out our hands."

"Man offers a woman something like that, looks like he could have a honeymooner's kiss, even if it was right in front of the family," Ben grumbled.

Everett laughed. These people didn't realize how funny the situation really was. "That's right, *cher. Laissez le bon temps rouler.*"

"What?" Maggie raised an eyebrow.

"That's . . . *honey, let the good times roll* in Cajun language." He opened up his arms. She could be honest and tell them, or by golly he could reap the benefits of such an outlandish offer (which he had no intentions of keeping).

Maggie walked into his arms. The kiss made the floor tremble—but not as much as Maggie's knees or Everett's heart.

Chapter Nine

Sun rays filtered through the gray skies, and the ever blowing Oklahoma wind had shifted to the south. The snow wouldn't last long, probably only until the morrow after all. Maggie stood on the front porch and waved at her family until they were out of sight. She sucked up another lungful of cold air and went in to face the music.

It was time she and Everett had a discussion. When it was over, she'd pack her few belongings, her four cats, and she'd go on up to Violet's place. Might as well let the whole story out now as later. She should have been honest from the first day and moved in with Violet. If she had, then there might have been an annulment after all, and Everett wouldn't have been forced to tell so blatant a lie. It was that very lie that brought Maggie to her senses. Something that should have never begun was now going on too long.

"Okay, let's get it over with, Everett," she said, marching through the door with resolve and determination. "I know you were lying about taking me to Georgia with you at Christmas. I might have done the same thing rather than face Daddy's temper today. But it was a lie all the same. I'm tired of lies. So I'm going to get my things together and move on up to Violet's place. The whole area is going to know in a few weeks that we are divorced anyway, so what's it matter?"

"So now I'm a liar as well as dull and a poor dancer," he said.

Maggie wished she had her father's gun right at that moment. Even the old blunderbuss shotgun. She could easily line up Everett's sexy eyes right in the sights and not even flinch when she pulled the trigger. To call him a mule-headed man would be doing a poor mule an injustice.

"I'm not going to fight with you," she said through clenched teeth. "I'm just leaving. You can tell everyone I left you. I don't care what they think. There's going to be talk no matter what or when. Might as well get it over with."

Everett Jackson Dulanis drew himself up to his full six feet and stood in front of the bedroom door, blocking her way. "Don't you call me a liar, Maggie," he said.

"Then don't be one," she said, pushing him; but he didn't budge. "Just get out of my way and let me get this job finished."

"I'm taking you to Georgia with me. We can both sign the papers, and you can leave from there. I will give you enough money to go wherever you want and you won't have to come back here, Maggie," he said.

"I told you in the beginning I didn't want your money, Everett," she said, her nose barely an inch from his.

He leaned forward and captured her mouth with his. It was an impulse that rattled his nerves as much as the cold kiss in the snow had done. "You earned it," he whispered hoarsely.

"I might have, but . . ." she said, wiping the heat from her mouth. Lord, it just wasn't fair for his kisses to make her knees weak like this. She turned her back to keep from wrapping her arms around his neck and dragging his lips down for another of those addictive kisses.

"But nothing. We'll go to Atlanta. James will have the papers all ready. We might have to go before the judge for a few minutes, but James assures me that it won't be anything but a formality. Then I'll come back here and tell folks that you've stayed on with my sister for a visit. By the time I tell them we are divorced you'll be elsewhere."

"Where would I go?" she whispered, fear creeping into her heart. Maggie had never been out on her own. She'd been poor, but there had been family and friends around her. She'd just assumed that she'd come back to Dodsworth and help Violet. But perhaps it would be better if she did go far, far away.

"I don't care where you go." Everett ran his fingertips through his hair and stomped across the floor to the window. Blasted woman anyway. Rubbing his kiss off her mouth before the warmth could even disappear. No woman had ever done that to him before. They might swoon but they sure never wiped the kiss away. He didn't know which angered him most. That she'd brush away his attentions or that just a mere kiss made him almost weak with desire.

It wasn't fair that his heart had fallen for Maggie. She was as ill suited to him as a, a . . . well, as a hog in a wallow, like he'd said in the beginning. Maggie should be a farmer's wife. Ivan Svenson would do just fine. He knotted his hands into fists and set his mouth in a firm line thinking about Ivan wrapping Maggie up in his big, Swedish arms on a cold night like this.

Everett determined that he would get over this. He'd gotten over Carolina quite well, and he could darn well do it again. However, Maggie was going with him to Georgia. It was now a battle of wills. That rotten empty shotgun had begun the marriage just the way her father demanded. Well, the whole marriage could finish the way Everett demanded.

"All right." Maggie stomped across the room even louder than he'd done. "All blasted right. I'll go to Georgia, but don't expect me to be like your sweet little Carolina, Everett, just because I'm in that state. I'm just Maggie and that's all I'll ever be. By the time we get the papers signed I'll decide where it is I want to go. And yes, I'll take enough of your money to get me there. That's payment for not embarrassing you by coming back to Dodsworth, I suppose. I don't like it, but it probably is the best way."

"Thank you," he said coldly. "We'll leave in three days. I will make the arrangements tomorrow. Just take a few things for yourself. I was serious when I said Eulalie would have seamstresses there. She mentioned it in her last letter. They will make you some new dresses."

Maggie's pride lay in a jumbled heap at her feet. She wasn't so senseless as to think her faded dresses would be acceptable in Atlanta, Georgia, on some big plantation. But then, neither would plain old Maggie. Everett might as well get used to the idea that putting fancy clothes on her wouldn't make her anything but a trumped up country clod.

The land sped by them at a breathtaking speed. Everett seemed oblivious to the grass going by in a blur or cows being in the window one minute and gone the next. It boggled Maggie's mind. She could scarcely believe that they could go so far from Oklahoma in only two days. In a wagon it would take weeks, not days. A herd of buffalo grazed not far from the train tracks and she wondered why they didn't run at the rumbling train running past them.

"They're used to it by now," Everett explained, reading her mind. Seeing a train ride from Maggie's eyes was exhilarating. No more than a dozen words had escaped her mouth since they'd first boarded and the porter had shown them down the narrow aisle way to their sleeper. Most of her words had been mere gasps or one syllable words at the most, but oh, her green eyes were sparkling with so much excitement that Everett wished he could gather it up in a basket and keep it close to his heart forever.

"How?" She never took her eyes away from the window.

"They've grown accustomed to the sounds and to the sight of the train every day. Probably several times a day," he explained.

She didn't answer. Everett knew everything. He was the

smartest man she'd ever known, but he had to be wrong. No animal or person either could ever get used to something so fabulous as riding on a train. Wherever she went when the divorce was over she fully well intended to go there on a train. She would scrub floors on her knees all year just to save money to ride a train somewhere every year.

They had boarded the train at mid morning. At noon she had scarcely blinked for fear she would miss something. Everett laid his book aside, stood up and stretched in the small place, paced a couple of times, and checked his gold pocket watch. "Lunch time, Maggie. Shall I catch the porter and have him bring us food in here or shall we go to the dining car?"

"Oh, Everett, could we really eat in the dining car?" She was breathless. Her eyes glittered. Her smile was infectious.

"Of course," he said, making a crook with his arm and holding it out to her.

She smoothed the front of her dress and slipped her arm through his. The sparks that flew didn't even surprise her. That she was attracted to her husband didn't shock her anymore. Little that it mattered anyway. James had sent a telegram saying that the judge would most likely grant the divorce without an appearance before him since it was holiday time. He was hoping to have everything finished by the day after Christmas. They would sign the papers and Everett would go back to Dodsworth and she'd go . . . where? She wouldn't think about it today. There were at least two whole weeks before Everett put money in her hand and sent her away. By then surely she'd know where she wanted to go.

The narrow aisle pressed them together tightly, but she didn't mind. For just a few minutes she was going to pretend she was really the wife of Dr. Everett Jackson Dulanis. For just one meal she was going to be someone other than plain old Maggie Listen.

At Everett's request the waiter seated them at a window

table and left them with leatherbound menus to choose from. Maggie's eyes swept down the list of items and gasped. "Oh, my, if I'd known things were so costly, I would have packed a picnic basket full of food for us. Everett, can you believe the price of a chicken salad sandwich?" She whispered so low he had to strain to hear her.

"Let me have that menu," he said, reaching across the table to take it from her. "I'll order for both of us."

"Food priced that high will make me sick," she stammered.

"Then don't think about it," he said, smiling.

"How can I not?" she asked.

"We'll have the special lunch." Everett ignored her remark and told the waiter who'd appeared at their table with a white towel draped over his arm and a pencil and paper to set down their order. "And for dessert, I think two fresh fruit cups. Strawberries and cantaloupe are in it?"

"Yes sir," the waiter nodded, "and peaches and bananas."

"That will be fine. And two glasses of sweet tea with lemon to drink," Everett added.

"Yes, sir. It will be about ten minutes," the waiter said and disappeared to the next table.

Maggie fingered the white linen table cloth and watched the couple across the car from them. The man reached across the table and took the lady's hands in his. They acted like they were the only people in the whole car. He stared deeply into her eyes and she smiled. Surely, they must be in love; perhaps even on their honeymoon.

"Penny for your thoughts, Maggie?" Everett leaned forward and whispered.

"I was thinking that it would be a grand thing to go on a honeymoon on a train. To sit at a fine table like this and order food off a menu and look deep into the eyes of someone that you loved and just let the train take you somewhere. Wouldn't matter where. Even if you just got on it and came right back when you reached the other end, it would be a grand thing for a honeymoon," she said.

Her words pricked his heart like the razor sharp edge of a two-edged sword. To Maggie, this was the greatest adventure of a lifetime. Wouldn't it be grand, as she'd said, to show her the world and see it through innocent, fresh eyes? Wouldn't it be even grander to see it through the eyes of love. It would never happen, though. He was just the dull, dumb doctor who couldn't dance and told an occasional lie to save his sorry hide.

"I thank you for taking me with you. Even if it is just so we can finally be separated legal-like, I still thank you, Everett. This is the best day of my life," Maggie said simply.

"You are quite welcome," he said past the lump in his throat.

"Your dinner, ma'am." The waiter set a plate before Maggie. Tiny little glazed carrots. Meat loaf, aromatic with onions and a curl of crispy bacon on the top. Mashed potatoes with a dollop of butter melting in the little well at the crest of the mound. A fresh salad of lettuce and tomatoes. Where did they ever get tomatoes in the middle of the winter? she wondered.

"Well, eat up before it gets cold." Everett shook out the napkin and laid it in his lap.

Maggie did the same, picked up a fork, and held it over the food for several moments. "I don't know what to taste first. It's too pretty to eat."

Everett chuckled. Train fare was far from scrumptious. At best it was palatable and kept body and soul stuck together from one point to the other. Even with the little curl of bacon, the meat loaf wouldn't taste nearly as good as Maggie's. The potatoes wouldn't be as rich with sweet cream, and even though there were real tomatoes on the top of the lettuce salad, they weren't as tasty as those from the garden.

"It's not funny," Maggie scolded him. "I'll try the carrots. Oh, Everett, they are delightful." She chewed slowly.

"But it is," he said. "It is very funny, Maggie. Because

I was just sitting here thinking that none of this is as good as what you make every day. The biscuit isn't as light. The meat loaf not nearly as tasty. And the tomatoes have very little flavor. Maybe the fruit cups will be better. I understand the train company buys fruit from the Rio Grande Valley in south Texas and their fruit is usually pretty good. I would have ordered pecan pie or chocolate cake, but you make those at home and the cooks here couldn't compare with yours."

"You've got to be crazy." Maggie shook her head. When she looked up from her plate, he had a faraway look in his eyes. A slight dimple in his left cheek deepened as he smiled at her. She'd never noticed that before. Maybe it only showed up when he was truly happy. Goodness only knew, he'd be happy when those papers were finally signed.

They visited the dining car again at supper time and Everett ordered a plain sandwich and soup for each of them. At nine o'clock the porter knocked softly on their door and asked if they were ready for him to turn down their beds. Everett merely nodded and went back to his book.

The view out the window had changed little through the day but now that it was dark, the stars and moon occupied her time. "I could have done that," she said when the porter was gone. "I never had a person turn down my bed before in my life. How are we going to manage this, Everett?"

"What?" He looked at the two berths.

"I mean, should I go out in the hall while you get undressed and into bed and then you turn your back?" she asked.

He reached behind her chair and pulled out a thin screen. A framework of wood with a fabric insert to keep it from being so heavy. "I think this might work. You go first. I've seen you lots of times in your gown when you come out and start the fire in the morning. When you are in bed I'll use the back side of the screen to get my pajamas on. You can have the bottom bunk."

"But the windows?"

He pulled a tassel on the side of the short drapes and they fell across the window, covering up Maggie's view. "I think that will work," he said.

"Okay," she said with a nod.

Fifteen minutes later they were both tucked in their narrow cot-like beds. The drapes were pulled, and they were two moths in cocoons. The rumble of the moving train usually lulled Everett right to sleep. Not so that night. Maggie was sleeping not three feet from him. He could practically hear her breathing. He could still smell the rose soap she used to bath her body in early that morning before they left the cabin. Every one of his senses were reeling and the knowledge of what that really meant was staggering. He couldn't bring himself to acknowledge any of it. He finally pounded his pillow into some kind of submission and willed himself to go to sleep.

It didn't work.

Maggie laid very still, the movement of the train making her think of sitting in her Momma's lap as a small child while her mother sang lullabies and rocked her to sleep. She shut her eyes. Visions of Everett filled the void. That faint little dimple in his cheek had appeared several times through the day. He'd laughed at the dinner table and again at supper. He'd make some lucky woman a fine husband someday. Yes, it was better that she wouldn't be going back to Dodsworth. It would break her heart to see that dimple deepen for another woman. She'd hugged her Momma very tightly, kissed Grace six times, and even hugged her father at the train station. She'd tell Elenor good-bye later, after she'd signed the papers and left Georgia permanently. Careful not to bump her head on the bunk above her, she sat up and fluffed her pillow into shape and laid her head on it. She'd think about Patches and the kittens she'd never see grow up, and fall right to sleep. It had been a long day full of experiences that she'd talk about the rest of her life. It was time to go to sleep and dream about train rides. She shut her eyes tightly and willed herself to go to sleep; right now.

It didn't work.

Eulalie and Jefferson waited on the platform. Her only brother, Everett Jackson was coming with his bride. Emma had written a long letter explaining the whole situation, and added that in her estimation they were living in the cabin together . . . in separate bedrooms.

The train came to a grinding halt, and Everett and a gorgeous red-haired beauty were the first two passengers to get off. Eulalie hollered his name and ran to hug him. It had been months since she'd seen him, and he'd never met her new babies. Two sons: Stuart and Montgomery. "You rascal, getting married and not even inviting us to the wedding," she said.

"Couldn't," he said, a grin lighting his face up like a candle in a dark house.

Maggie's heart fell in a pulsating ball of aching pain at her feet. Eulalie was the most gorgeous woman she'd ever seen. Dark hair, dark eyes, translucent skin, a body that surely hadn't borne twin sons just a few months ago. She was dressed in a fashionable, navy blue skirt with a lovely silky blouse. A short matching velvet cape with fur trim flipped back over her shoulders as she hugged her brother. No wonder Everett had said she was as suited to be his wife as a sow in a wallow. That's exactly what she felt like right at that moment in her best dark green cotton dress and her faded wool coat.

"And you must be Maggie." Eulalie turned her brightest smile toward her new sister-in-law. "I'm so glad to finally meet you. We are going to be great friends as well as sisters. Come and meet Jefferson. He's overseeing getting your baggage into our carriage. I'm so glad you could come a week early. We'll get to know each other before Emma and the horde get here. Just think, her five and our two. Seven children. Who knows? We could have even more next Christmas." She winked conspiratorially at Maggie, who blushed as red as her hair. "Wouldn't it be something if you and Everett Jackson had twins, too?"

"Not very likely," Maggie managed to mutter as Eulalie grabbed her hand and led her toward the most magnificent buggy Maggie had ever seen.

"I took the liberty of ordering fabrics for new Christmas finery," Eulalie chattered on the way to the plantation.

Maggie just nodded, trying to get a hold of something that didn't absolutely bewilder her at that moment. Everett and Jackson were deep into a conversation about cotton, tobacco, and sugar plantations. Jefferson scarcely looked old enough to be Emma's father. His hair was still dark and his eyes still young. Maybe being married to the vivacious Eulalie did that for him.

"Emma wrote that you had strange-colored hair," Eulalie said. "She said it was the color of a burgundy leaf from a black maple tree in the fall. So I had one of the stable boys gather me up several leaves and took them with me to order the fabric. I figured you'd be lovely in pink and now that I see you, I don't doubt it."

"Pink?" Maggie stammered. "But Momma said I had to wear green. I've always loved pink, but . . ."

"But nothing. I selected a green, too. For morning tea with some of the local ladies. But for the Christmas party, you are wearing pink velvet trimmed in silver embroidery. Emma had a dress made for mine and Jefferson's engagement party that I thought we'd copy. It's quite simple and yet elegant. You can make the final decisions though. I do tend to take over," Eulalie said.

"That's all right," Maggie said. "I'm sure you know more than I do about things like that."

Eulalie saw the pain in Maggie's face. The humiliation. It broke Eulalie's heart. Here sat the most beautiful woman her brother had ever shown interest in. Carolina Prescott's blonde beauty paled in comparison to Maggie. And the girl didn't even know she was pretty. Everett Jackson was going to get a healthy dose of his sister's controlling nature and wicked tongue as soon as she got him alone. He should have already convinced Maggie of her worth and beauty. And he surely should have burned that horrid coat Maggie drew around her tightly, trying no doubt to cover the faded green cotton dress she wore.

Jefferson and Everett scarcely looked up when the carriage stopped. They were discussing something about a letter from Everett's overseer saying the sugar crop was the best ever at his plantation in Louisiana. "Don't pay any attention to them," Eulalie laughed. "Menfolks talk as much about crops as us women do about our fabrics. Come inside, *cher,* and meet my sons."

"Our sons! And I heard that comment, darlin'." Jefferson patted her on the fanny as he helped her out of the carriage. "We might talk about crops but our thoughts aren't far from our women, are they?" He winked at Everett.

"No sir," Everett said honestly. "Now where are these nephews of mine?"

"In the nursery waiting for us." Eulalie dragged them into the house.

Maggie wanted to stop and stare her fill of the foyer where a butler removed their coats and took them to another room. A huge gold-framed mirror hung above a credenza with a fresh flower arrangement and a silver tray with several cards lying on it. Scarlet velvet chairs flanked a small table with a silver coffee service in the middle. Steam rising from the pot attested to the fact that it was indeed used often.

"I see you eyeing that coffee," Eulalie said gracefully. "Here. I'll pour you a cup to warm you up. We'll have lunch in a few minutes. We'll take the coffee with us upstairs to see the boys. You want some, Everett Jackson?"

"Of course. Is it strong?"

"Enough to curl your toe nails and straighten your hair. With just a little chicory added to give it some body." She laughed.

"Then of course I want a cup," Everett said. "Maggie takes hers black, too, by the way."

Eulalie poured. Maggie sipped the coffee and rolled her green eyes toward the vaulted ceiling. It was absolutely the best coffee she'd ever tasted. Maybe she'd choose a place somewhere where they served coffee like this, to live forever. She followed Maggie up the wide curving staircase.

"Our sons," Eulalie slung open the door. Two identical little boys sat on a pallet with a teenage girl who was reading them a book about a little green snake. They both had dark hair and blue eyes, and Maggie could tell even at their young age, they'd keep the female population in Atlanta vying for their attentions when they got older.

Someday she'd have sons. Lots of them. Someday when she found a man who looked at her with all the love Jefferson Cummins had in his eyes when he looked at Eulalie.

"They're beautiful." Maggie handed her empty cup to Everett, gathered up her skirt tails, and sat down on the pallet. Both boys reached for her at the same time. She made a lap big enough to accommodate both their chubby bodies.

"Well?" Eulalie turned to Everett.

"They are too pretty for boys," he said, grinning. "You'll have your hands full, my sister."

"Not as full as you will if Maggie makes twin girls who look like her. She's gorgeous, Everett. And we will talk later about your lack of taking care of matters properly," she whispered so low Maggie couldn't hear her.

"We'll talk later about the reasons for that," he said.

"You bet we will," Eulalie said tersely.

Chapter Ten

Maggie had been agog at the foyer and the curving staircase up to the bedrooms on the second floor, but she was absolutely amazed at the room she was given to freshen up in before lunch. She found her best green dress, the one she'd worn the night she and Everett wound up in trouble, along with the rest of her things already unpacked and hanging in the shiny cherry wardrobe. She ran the tip of her finger across the beautiful wood and sighed. Not even in Emma's or Violet's house had she seen such a lovely room.

The maid who showed her to the room after they left the little boy's nursery politely nodded toward the door across the room and told her that was the entrance to the suite where her husband Dr. Everett would be sleeping at night. As if Maggie would care about that. The door might as well be nailed shut with ten penny nails and a bar put across each side. Everett Jackson Dulanis would never be her husband. Not on anything but paper.

Behind that door Everett picked up a washcloth, dipped it in cool water and held it against his eyes. He'd heard the old adage about weaving tangled webs when a person practiced deceit. But he and Maggie had told the truth and look what a tangled web they were in. Right beyond the door was the woman his heart had begun to crave; his eyes sought out whenever she wasn't beside him; his fingertips longed to touch. And he wasn't good enough for her. She didn't care a tinker's dam about him being a prominent doctor. Wouldn't even bat an eye if he took her to the family sugar plantation in Louisiana and showed her exactly what he was worth. He couldn't dance to suit her and he wasn't full of laughs and giggles, so Maggie couldn't be bothered with him.

A slight knock brought his eyes to the door connecting his room with the one they'd given Maggie. Surely not? A faint smile played at the corners of his mouth and he had his hand on the door knob when his sister slipped in the other door from the hallway.

"Okay, Everett Jackson." She raised an eyebrow. "I want some answers."

"Then ask the questions," he said, the smile replaced with a haunting look that didn't get past his older sister.

"Why does your wife look like a cleaning lady? And why isn't she at least wearing a plain gold wedding band. For goodness sakes, Everett Jackson, she was supposed to get Momma's wedding ring. The one with a big emerald surrounded by diamonds. I could see you'd have to take her to Sweet Penchant to get the ring as well as the rest of the jewelry but good grief, she could have decent clothing and a gold ring," Eulalie whispered.

"We aren't staying married. It was all a mistake." Everett sat down in an overstuffed chair beside the balcony doors. "I would have never given her a second look. She's the . . . well, it's hard to explain, *cher.* She's not the shiniest knife in the drawer. Folks in Dodsworth just smile at Maggie. The only thing she ever cared about is dancing. But once you get to know her, she's got so much depth it's scary. Then she'll turn right around and want to build a snowman. She's a complex woman that everyone dubbed slow because they don't understand her. She's got a heart of gold."

"You haven't answered my questions," Eulalie said, feeling her brother's bewildered pain.

"She won't have anything new from me. She's too proud. I never thought of a ring because we never intended to be married even this long. She wants out of this as badly as I do. Let me explain. We were at a country dance. The last one of the year. The barn was out away from anyone's house and a storm came up. Everyone scattered. Her father had brought two wagons of people and she ran back inside at the last minute to get something she'd left behind. When she got back outside everyone was gone. Each wagon load of her friends thought she was with the other one. Like a gentleman I offered to take her home. Only the lightning spooked the horse and my buggy ended up turned over. We found an old dugout house and a couple of blankets that had been left behind. We shucked out of our drenched clothes, wrapped up in the blankets while they dried, and fell asleep. That's the way her father and his shotgun found us the next day. She doesn't want to be married to a dull doctor who can't dance the country dances. I don't want a wife like Maggie."

"Then why didn't you just have it annulled?"

"Tried. James said it has to be a divorce since she lived with me. There wasn't any place else for her to go and . . ."

Eulalie bit the inside of her lip to keep from laughing. Suddenly she remembered the meddling Jed's Aunt Beulah did back when Emma and Jed couldn't find each other in the massive storms in their hearts. Was it her turn to meddle? If it was, she was surely up to the task. She'd have a whole beaucoup of questions for Emma when she arrived in a few days. When she got the answers, the meddling would most definitely begin.

"Have you fallen in love with your wife?" Eulalie asked bluntly.

"It wouldn't do me a bit of good to be in love with Maggie. She doesn't want me. Isn't that a hoot, *cher?* She doesn't care what kind of man she has for a husband, so long as he makes her laugh and he can dance. Wealth doesn't mean anything to her. Poverty is all she's ever known and she'll embrace it with open arms for the rest of her life, if the man will just fit those two bills," Everett said.

"Sounds like the rest of the population in your Indian Territory is touched. Not our Maggie. Sounds to me like she's got more brains than most women I know. Lunch is in fifteen minutes, then you and Jefferson are scheduled for a tour. He's looked forward to your visit and he wants to show you what he's doing with the small patch of sugar cane he's experimenting with. I'll see you down stairs in a few minutes?"

"Yes, *cher.* I'm just going to sit for a moment and rest my tired eyes." He tried to smile, but his dimple didn't deepen.

Maggie sat up with a start when someone knocked on her door. She'd only meant to stretch out for a moment on the beautiful white bedspread. She hadn't intended to shut her eyes or fall asleep. She looked across the room at the door between her room and Dr. Everett's. What could he be wanting? To tell her not to expect to stay married to him now that they were away from Dodsworth and she could see exactly what kind of life he led? Well, he could drop graveyard dead if he thought for one minute she'd change her mind. Besides, even if she did listen to her heart, Everett Dulanis could never be her true husband. Because he didn't love Maggie. And that was even more important than a man who'd make her laugh or even one who could dance longer and better than she could. She would not be married to any man who just flat didn't love her—Maggie Listen—just the way she was.

She was still staring at the door when the door out into the hallway opened just a crack and Eulalie poked her head inside. "I'm sorry, *cher.* Were you asleep?"

"No, just resting my eyes a moment," Maggie said, smiling. "Come right in."

Eulalie stepped into the room. Maggie was absolutely breathtaking even in her faded cotton dress. She was a bit taller than Eulalie but built on the same frame. A slight bit top heavy, tiny waist, delicate features, and the most mysterious deep green eyes Eulalie had ever seen. They were the color of Louisiana moss on the shady side of the tree with the sun rays dancing around it, yet not touching the color to lighten it. All that gorgeous burgundy red hair, no freckles, and translucent skin would make any man's heart run away like a steam engine.

"Lunch is in fifteen minutes and then the seamstresses arrive right after that. I just asked my brother about your marriage and he told me you two are not staying married. Do you not love him?" Eulalie asked the loaded question and watched Maggie's expression as much as listened to her words.

"It wouldn't matter if I loved him, Eulalie," Maggie looked at her shoes. "Dr. Everett Dulanis deserves a wife with class. One who knows how to act and behave like a doctor's wife. I'm just plain old Maggie. Most folks even laugh behind my back and say I'm sort of simple minded. They think I'm daft and that I don't know what they say, but I do. Everett deserves much more than that. He's the smartest man I've ever known. He needs a wife to match him, not one that would drag him down. When Carolina came and found us living in the same house, he went running into town to talk to her. He said I was as suited to him as a hog in a wallow. It made me mad at first, but since then I've come to realize he was just speaking the truth. It's for the best that we go our separate ways. James will have the papers ready in a few days. We'll sign them and I'm going off somewhere far away. It's best I don't live in Dodsworth where I'd be an embarrassment to him."

"I see," Eulalie said. "Well, we've got a full two weeks ahead of us. Maybe I can help you decide where you want to go. You know, Atlanta is a big place. But then so is the Crooked Oaks. We might find a place for you here."

"I don't think so," Maggie said. "If you got ideas I'd be willin' to listen. But I won't stay anyplace where I'd have to see him again, Eulalie. Wouldn't be no use in causing myself even more hurt. Now can I help with lunch?"

"No, *cher,* the cook will take care of that. But you can come and see the fabrics in the sewing room. Five seamstresses are coming from Atlanta and staying a whole week with us. You aren't going to be able to do much more than eat and go to fittings," Eulalie said lightheartedly.

"Oh, my." Maggie's eyes widened. "But I don't need . . ."

"Neither do I, but I'm having." Eulalie laughed and grabbed her hand to lead her across the hallway and up to the loft where the sewing would soon begin.

Eulalie had heard from both sides. Neither had said that they didn't love the other one, but rather that the other one wasn't in love. Sounded a bit like a heartbreak on the way to the judge's quarters. But then there was always meddling. Aunt Beulah accomplished her feat from all those miles away. Eulalie was right there with both of them and she wasn't without her wiles.

Eulalie led the way to the long lofty room with sunlight pouring in from two doors out onto the widow's walk. Bolts and bolts of fabric lined the walls. More material than Duncan had in his whole store, and richer fabrics. Of course, no one in Dodsworth would have a need for plush dusty pink velvet. Maggie reached out and buried her finger tips in the soft nap of the velvet.

"It's so pretty," she said.

"It's the piece I thought of for you right away. I think a few fleur-de-lis embroidered in silver thread around the neckline would be elegant. A straight dress like the one Emma wore only with a very short train at the back. Maybe long fitted leg-o-mutton sleeves." Eulalie picked up the bolt of material and wound off yards and yards to wrap around Maggie.

"Oh, my." Maggie laughed. A rich, true laugh born in her chest and erupting in honesty.

"Look," Eulalie said, turning her to face a floor-length mirror on the wall behind her. Maggie gasped. She'd never seen her whole self at one time in a real mirror. Maybe in the reflection of the creek if the light was just right. But there she was, wrapped in a cocoon of dusty pink velvet. Was that really simple Maggie staring back at her?

"Lovely," Eulalie whispered in her soft southern voice. "We are going to have so much fun, my sister. I never had a sister before. I didn't tell you that, yet, did I. There was just me and Everett Jackson. He wouldn't stand still for me to dress him in pink velvet."

That vision brought on a case of giggles Maggie had trouble containing.

Eulalie giggled with her as she unwrapped the velvet. "Our men folks are probably waiting. We'll come back and play after the seamstresses get here, *cher.*"

"But Eulalie, we aren't really sisters. Because Everett and I aren't really married, and what there is, is about to end," Maggie said seriously.

"We'll see." Eulalie hooked her arm in Maggie's and led her down the staircases to the dining room where the men waited. Yes, just as Eulalie thought, sparks danced all around the room when Everett looked up and saw his wife enter the room.

Let the meddling begin!

Chapter Eleven

Maggie dressed in a crispy green taffeta creation with a high rounded neckline, fitted waist and bustled back and trimmed with forest green velvet cuffs and collar. The fine cotton of her undergarments felt like silk against her skin. The seamstresses had performed sheer miracles in the past two days since Emma, Jed, and Elenor had arrived in a flurry of excitement and children.

The plantation had no trouble holding the children, who found new wonders every which way they turned. But it almost burst at the seams when Emma announced the day after their arrival that she'd caught Elenor and James on their way to the courthouse to elope. No, that would never do. Ben and Iris Listen, back in Dodsworth, would never forgive Emma if she didn't give them some kind of wedding. So here they were two days later, the living room decorated beautifully in poinsettias and red velvet bows and a wedding about to take place.

A proper wedding. The kind Maggie had always envisioned for herself. Maybe not an elaborate one like Elenor was about to have, but one where the groom loved the bride and the bride was so besotted she didn't even care about a wedding but rather wanted to be his wife. Maggie picked up her bouquet of white poinsettias and crossed the hallway to the room where Elenor was sitting for Emma to finish fixing her blonde hair.

"So are we about ready?" Maggie asked.

"Oh, Maggie, look at you. You are beautiful!" Elenor gasped.

"Oh, hush up, you'll have me weeping." Maggie brushed the comment aside. Of course Elenor would say that. She was in love and everything was beautiful, and besides she was her sister.

"Emma, her hair is lovely," Maggie said. "Let's get her shoved down in all those layers of white lace, now. Mercy, Momma wouldn't believe this dress. I can't wait until you write and tell me what she says about it when you try it on for her back in Dodsworth."

"Whatever are you talking about?" Elenor asked. "You'll be right there to see her face."

"Oh, I don't know. You and James might get there before me," Maggie covered her words. Lord, she'd have to be more careful. She wouldn't do anything to spoil her sister's wedding day. Not if it meant biting her tongue off at the root.

"I doubt it," Elenor smiled. "We're staying here for six months or so until he can get all his affairs in order. That's after we go to Louisiana for a couple of weeks. Oh, Maggie, can you believe us Listen girls are marrying up with doctors and lawyers. I wouldn't care what James did. He could shoe horses the rest of our lives and we could live in a dugout so long as I could be with him. That's why we decided to go ahead and get married now. We can't bear being apart."

"Step easy now." Maggie held the dress for her sister.

"Oh, its so lovely," Elenor said when she stood before the mirrors. "I wish Violet could see this dress."

"So do I," Maggie whispered, staring at her younger sister. "Well, I suppose it's time, now."

"Yes, it is." Emma looked up as the clock chimed six times in the foyer. "I hear Eulalie beginning to play the piano. Give me two minutes to get down there and sit down. I'll go by the back stairs. Then you go, Maggie. Move slowly down the stairs."

Maggie picked up the bouquet. At the top of the stairs she looked down and saw Everett standing at the front of the room full of filled chairs. James was beside him, and the preacher waited with them. She gasped and pasted on a smile. What she wouldn't give to be a bride instead of a matron-of-honor that day couldn't be measured in dollars and cents. James fidgeted nervously; but Everett was a pillar of steel.

He didn't know how Maggie saw him, but just looking at her so regally descending the stairs made his insides quiver with desire. She was a vision from a fashion magazine in that strange green rustling dress trimmed in a darker velvet. Her dark red hair was piled high on her head and had some kind of wispy white flowers strewn in it. He wished she was the bride and he was the nervous groom—but wishes weren't granted in his world.

Elenor was lovely when she started down the stairs in all that bridal white lace. But she'd never hold a candle to Maggie's beauty, Everett thought as he listened to his best friend exchange wedding vows with his bride. To think that he'd been ready to beg and plead with James to think again before he married the girl was almost funny right then. They were so suited to one another it was uncanny. Elenor brought out the best in his lifelong friend, and goodness only knew he'd certainly made her eyes light up with happiness. Everett wanted nothing more than to stare his fill of his own wife during the ceremony, but every time he looked across at her, she was staring back at him. It made him uncomfortable, knowing that she wanted to run out of their marriage with as much fervor as Elenor wanted to run into hers with James.

Well, it wouldn't be long now. James had brought the papers with him to the wedding. After it was all over and before he and Elenor went to Louisiana for a honeymoon in Terrebonne County, they'd take a moment to step into the library and put their names on the right lines. Everett would have to take the papers to the courthouse and file them so it would be legal, but that wouldn't be a big job. And then Maggie would be rid of the man who couldn't dance and wouldn't laugh.

"By the authority vested in me by the state of Georgia and God, Almighty, I now pronounce you man and wife." The preacher finished the ceremony. "Now, James, you may kiss the bride."

Maggie wondered if Elenor felt the same jolt shock her body when James kissed her that she'd felt when Everett's lips touched hers those two times. She sincerely hoped so.

A reception complete with a three-tiered wedding cake followed the ceremony. James had just finished feeding Elenor the first bite of cake and the band was gearing up to play when Maggie felt a presence at her elbow. She turned quickly to see if Everett was there and stared right into Carolina's blue eyes.

"So you refused to let him go when you found out his worth," she said snippily in a voice barely above a whisper.

"You don't know what you're talking about," Maggie said softly. "I understand you are having a New Year's wedding. I wish you the best."

"A pretty dress can't cover up what a woman really is," Carolina said behind a smile.

"You ought to know," Maggie said and moved toward her sister to hug her one more time.

Everett raised his punch cup in a salute to the newly wedded couple. As best man he was responsible for the first toast. "To my friend, James and his new wife, Elenor. I have to admit I was on the verge of trying to talk him out of getting married, but I also have to admit I was wrong. They are a perfect couple. Here's to them and to all the happiness a lifetime can heap upon their heads," he said, looking right at Maggie.

Two hours later, Elenor slipped away from James and

asked Maggie to please help her change into her traveling outfit. She and James were about to leave for their first night in James's Atlanta house. The next day they would travel to Louisiana for a couple of weeks. "Oh, Maggie, I'm so happy I could cry," Elenor said as her sister buttoned up the back of her dark blue traveling dress.

"Well, I should hope so," Maggie said.

"Did you feel like this that first day?" Elenor asked.

"Hardly. Our circumstances were a little different. That shotgun didn't wear a pretty green dress, you know?" Maggie laughed.

"But you feel this way now. I can see it when you look at Everett and he couldn't keep his eyes off you during the ceremony. He sure does love you, Maggie." Elenor slung a new floor-length cape over her dress and hugged Maggie for the hundredth time. "Please write Momma a long letter and tell her all about the wedding. I sent a telegram telling them I was marrying James and staying here. But you could tell her all about the dresses and tell her I love her. And when you get home, go see her and tell her again."

"I'll sure write her," Maggie said, tears dripping on her broken heart since she refused to let them flow down her cheeks.

They left in a carriage with everyone waving from the porch. Friends, family, and hired help, all alike in their wishes for a long and happy life for the couple. Maggie stayed long past when everyone else went back into the house. She needed time to sort out the feelings in her heart. The pain. The happiness. All of it wound tightly and choking the life from her. She wrapped her new cape around her shivering body and walked toward Eulalie's gardens. The roses were dormant right now and nothing more than sticks, but that didn't matter to Maggie. She just needed space between her own feelings and the crowd of people still dancing and enjoying themselves in the house.

Not one time had Everett asked her to dance with him. She'd danced with Jefferson, with James, even with Carolina's intended, a handsome man named Gatlin. Maggie couldn't for the very life of her figure that one out: what it was Gatlin had that would make him rate above Everett Dulanis. Carolina must be as senseless as most folks thought Maggie was.

"But please . . ." Maggie heard a plaintive whisper coming from the deep shadows of an evergreen tree. She stopped and turned around to walk another way when she recognized Everett's voice.

"I couldn't do that to my best friend," he said hoarsely.

"But I've made a mistake, darling. I was so angry with you for moving to that wilderness. I can't possibly live there, Everett. But I still love you. Gatlin will just have to understand. Kiss me darling. Let me show you how much I love you," Carolina said.

Maggie watched the two shadows move closer together.

"Carolina, I cannot. Gatlin is my friend. I . . ."

"You will," she demanded. "Or I'll go in the house and tell everyone there you compromised me out here. I'll tell them that you begged me to go outside with you. If I have to, I'll tear the bodice from my dress and swear you did it. I won't marry him, Everett. I'll have you one way or the other."

"Carolina, listen to reason," Everett said.

"Kiss me and I'll listen to you tell me how lovely I am and that you never stopped loving me," she cooed.

"I think not," Maggie said in a loud voice as she plowed right between the two of them and wrapped her arms around Everett's waist. "You better take yourself on back in the house through the back door. I'm sure your intended is searching for you for a dance, Carolina. But you will not compromise my husband or make a problem for him in any way—or I'll take care of it. Do you understand me?"

"You wouldn't dare," Carolina sneered.

"I would," Maggie said, trying to still her quivering insides at the mere touch of Everett so close to her. "You might be surprised what this country clod in a fancy dress would do to someone who threatened her husband. I might tell the whole county what you just said and ruin your reputation. I might take you down and whup your fine southern rear end right here in the dirt. You see, I can do anything I want. I have nothing to lose in this place."

"You are nothing but a trumped up harlot. If you hadn't slept with him this wouldn't be happening." Carolina stamped her foot and pointed at Maggie.

Maggie slapped her hand away. "That's the pot calling the kettle black, I'd say. You're out here with another woman's husband trying to get him to kiss you while your intended is in the house hunting for you and *you* call *me* a harlot. Go back in the house before your big mouth gets you in more trouble than you can get out of."

"Okay, ladies, let's all just go in the house and pretend this never happened," Everett said.

"Hummph," Carolina stuck her nose in the air and ran back toward the porch. "You can both go back to that nasty place you came from and I hope you rot there together."

"Oh, no!" Everett exclaimed.

"What now?" Maggie said, drawing away from him reluctantly.

"James and Elenor got away and we didn't sign the papers. He had them in his case and we were supposed to slip away for a minute. Then Carolina came to me begging for a moment of privacy and . . ."

"And we can scarcely go running after them on their first night together," Maggie said. "They leave tomorrow morning at dawn for Louisiana, you know."

Everett groaned. Another two weeks. Would the fates never work in his favor?

"I'm sorry, Everett. I truly am. I know how you wanted this to be over," Maggie said, sympathetically. "Let's go back inside before Carolina causes more problems."

"Thank you for taking care of that," Everett said, wishing he could draw Maggie back into his arms again.

"Just a little cat fight. She'd just better be careful. Her

citified claws are a little dull compared to my old rough country claws. Now let's go back inside," she said.

"On one condition," Everett said. "That you dance the rest of the dances with me. I'm afraid my sister is going to have me drawn and quartered for letting all the other men dance with the prettiest girl at the wedding."

For the first time in her life, Maggie Listen was totally speechless.

Chapter Twelve

Eulalie had promised that the Christmas party wasn't a big affair. But a hundred people was surely a big to-do to Maggie. That was as many or more people than attended a summer barn dance in Logan County, and here they were all going to be in the house. She'd arranged greenhouse flowers in silver and crystal vases all day. She'd helped Emma put icing on the cake Eulalie wanted used for the centerpiece on the refreshment table. She'd dressed carefully in the pink dress with silver embroidery. Now all she had to do was put on her gloves and walk down the staircase with Everett.

Eulalie and Jefferson would greet the guests at the door as they arrived. Emma and Jed were to appear at the top of the stairs at exactly five minutes past seven. The band would stop playing and in the silence everyone would watch them descend. Five minutes later, after Emma and Jed had danced a slow waltz, Maggie and Everett were to appear at the top of the stairs.

It didn't seem like so much at the time. Almost regal. But standing there waiting on Everett to knock on one of the doors in her bedroom was trying her nerves. That's not what he wanted in Georgia at all. To have Maggie presented to everyone as his real wife. No, he, like Maggie, had expected to spend a quiet holiday with his family and get this divorce business over with.

A gentle knock came from the door out into the hallway. They'd both ignored the door separating their bedrooms. It might as well have been a solid wall. She opened the door and pulled on her gloves as Everett waited without entering her sanctuary. His mouth was dry when he looked at Maggie in her finest gown of the season. If he'd had to produce enough saliva to swallow or face a firing squad, he'd would have just put the blindfold on his eyes and waited for the click of the rifles. The dusty pink brought a glow to her cheeks. Go back a hundred years and she could have modeled for one of the great masters.

"You are very lovely tonight, *cher,*" he said when his tongue came unglued from the roof of his mouth.

"I'm just Maggie in a new dress. But thank you, Everett." She smiled. Once when he was a small boy he'd found a bed of moss just the color of her eyes and growing along side it was a patch of some kind of wild pink flowers almost the same color as that dress. The silver embroidery reminded him of the sun rays sneaking through the cypress trees and dancing around the moss and flowers.

"You don't look so shabby yourself, Everett," she said, bracing herself for the shock when she slipped her hand through his looped arm. "Just hope the plain old Maggie inside this fancy frock doesn't fall on her face going down those stairs."

He threw back his head and laughed. Plain old Maggie sure had a way of stating things delightfully. Looking back at her homilies and simplicity, he wondered why he'd ever found her plain in any sense of the word.

Everett had laughed. His dimples were deep. His brown eyes sparkled. All at the thought of her falling flat on her face. Maggie set her jaw in anger. "Well, I didn't mean for such a vision to bring you so much pleasure. Would you have laughed so hard at Carolina sprawled out at the bottom of the steps with her drawers showing to the whole world?" she snapped.

He laughed again. "Maggie, *cher,* I was not visualizing any such thing. It was the fact that you referred to yourself as plain. You'd run the fashion queens in New York stiff competition, and you are so naive that you don't even know it. Come, let's make our grand entrance. Every man in the place is going to be jealous of Everett Jackson Dulanis tonight."

Shyness erased any sassy remark from her mind. So he actually thought she was pretty. And he had laughed. He really was a good dancer at the dances they did in more refined society. It'd take a long time before he could really throw caution to the Oklahoma wind and dance with no inhibitions, but she had to admit he could waltz beautifully. Why did she fight against being married to him? That was easy to answer. Maggie wouldn't be married to someone who didn't love her. As much as James loved Elenor. Enough to elope at the courthouse just to be together for all eternity. Yet, enough to wait a while so she could have a proper wedding. Maggie would have that or she'd live on the memories of this fantastic time in her life for all eternity. She'd open the chest she'd already planned to put the gloves and the pink dress inside and touch them. She'd close her green eyes and see Everett again in his fine black suit. With his dimple deepened in happiness. While her eyes were closed she'd take a deep breath and smell the wonderful aroma of Christmas as they made their way down the hallway, as the music played. She'd have the memories to keep her.

Everett stopped midway down the hallway. The music was still playing. Eulalie said they were to appear at the top of the stairs when the music stopped. He looked down on Maggie's deep red hair at the same time she looked up at him. The kiss that came next was as natural as if they'd truly been married. He bent slightly. She tiptoed and their lips met somewhere in the middle. Their hearts raced with a head of steam. Their bodies were glued to the floor.

Maggie wanted the kiss to never end. It would be one more bittersweet memory to add to her growing collection. Three kisses and a pink dress. Was that enough to hold her through the rest of her life? It would have to be, because she'd never settle for anything else now.

The last thing Everett wanted to do was take Maggie down the stairs to the party. He'd much rather have picked her up and carried her back to his bedroom. A dozen more steamy kisses wouldn't be enough to satisfy his hunger. But Everett Jackson Dulanis was a serious doctor who could never harness the free spirit of Maggie Laura Listen.

The music stopped, as did the kiss on the same note. Without a word, Everett steered them toward the top of the stairs, where he pasted on a smile that didn't reach his sad eyes. The high color that filled Maggie's cheeks had nothing to do with reflections from the pink and silver in her gown. If she hadn't been wearing gloves she would have touched her lips again, just to see if they were as hot as they felt.

In the sudden silence, everyone looked up again. Maggie stepped even slower than she'd done at the wedding. Everett nodded at the people but kept his eyes on Maggie. In the short time they had left together he'd never get enough pictures of her branded in his mind and on his heart. If only . . . but if only wasn't his to have. Not then. Not ever.

Carolina and Gatlin were the first couple waiting at the bottom of the staircase. They surely had not planned it that way, but when the last dance ended and the music stopped, it found them there. Carolina smiled brightly at Everett and ignored Maggie. Gatlin extended his hand.

"Hello, again, my friend," Everett said. "Are you getting settled in this fair city?"

"Yes, I am," Gatlin said, still amazed that Everett harbored no hard feelings. But then why should he, when he had someone as lovely and honest as Maggie for a wife.

The music started at that moment and Everett nodded toward Carolina. "I must dance this waltz with my wife, so if you will excuse us. We'll visit later."

Eulalie watched them dance from the sidelines. They were meant for each other. Maggie with her simple outlook on life to temper the seriousness of her brother. The way Maggie looked up at him and hung on every word almost wrung tears from Eulalie's heart. They were both so much in love. It didn't take an intelligent person to know that. But getting them to acknowledge it and say so was worse than pulling hen's teeth.

"You have adapted to the city dances very well, Maggie," Everett said, drawing her closer than was appropriate, even for married couples.

"And you do very well at this kind of dancing," Maggie said.

"Oh? Does that mean you are retracting your opinion of me not being able to dance?" Everett said.

"Excuse me," Gatlin tapped Everett on the shoulder. "Shall we change, my friend?"

Everett could have gladly planted his fist between Gatlin's eyes. Just when he and Maggie were warming up to one another he had to give her up to polite society. He stepped back, and there was Carolina with her arms outstretched waiting for him to take Gatlin's spot. Forget hitting the man. Everett could have pulled out a shotgun and shot him.

"Have you changed your mind since you've had time to think about things without your trashy wife around?" Carolina whispered as they circled the floor together.

"Don't call my wife names. She's one of the finest women you'll ever know, Carolina. There's not a mean bone in her body," Everett said.

"She's not the woman for you, Everett. I am. I'll call the wedding off to Gatlin right up to the last minute. Just tell me you'll start a practice in New York or even in Baton Rouge. Anywhere but back in those sticks where you've been hiding. You said you were getting a divorce. You promised me that at the train station that day. Well, I have decided that maybe I will wait until it is final," Carolina all but purred.

"No thank you," Everett said.

The music ended and Gatlin brought Maggie back to Everett's side. "She dances as well as she is beautiful. You have chosen well in a wife," Gatlin said.

"Thank you. I believe I have," Everett said. "Would you care for punch, Maggie?"

"I would," Carolina said, hating Gatlin for that comment. He'd pay for it later. No kisses for him tonight, and he'd better find a place that sold roses in the winter time before he came begging for one the next day.

"Then let's go get these ladies some punch," Gatlin said. "You two wait right here and don't let any of these men talk you into a dance."

"We wouldn't dream of it." Carolina smiled. "Did you dig that dress out of Eulalie's Halloween costume trunk?" she said when the men were out of hearing distance.

"How did you guess?" Maggie laughed. So she'd rankled the witch with her dress. Carolina wore a clear red taffeta with layers and layers of gold edged lace, a wide sweeping skirt and the biggest bustle Maggie had ever seen.

"Oh, I never forget a dress. Emma wore that one when she was pretending to be Napoleon's wife," Carolina said. "And pink with your hair. It's horrid."

Maggie smiled. "Well, darlin', you look wonderful tonight. It's evident you didn't have to drag your frock out of a trunk. Someone has made it special for you just so you light up your intended's eyes tonight. My, oh my, the way he looks at you, why a body would think he could have you for breakfast. It's amazin' to me how you could ever want to throw him over for a backwoods doctor like Everett. Goodness only knows someone fancy as you are wouldn't ever fit in amongst those of us in Dodsworth who are just happy to have a Halloween trunk to go through for a party dress."

"Are you two getting to know each other?" Gatlin put a crystal punch cup in Carolina's hand.

"Why of course we are, sir," Maggie said. "I was just admiring her lovely Christmas frock."

"Well, your evening gown is stunning. Looks like you stepped out of some fancy modeling book," Gatlin said.

"Thank you." Maggie took the cup of red punch from Everett's hand and sipped on it. Another memory. One of crushed strawberries in the middle of the winter.

"It should be stunning. I've scarcely seen the women folks in this house all week. Eulalie hired about a half a dozen seamstresses and they've been sewing from dawn to midnight every day. Just the embroidery on this creation took two days of constant work, according to Emma, who's teased me unmercifully about how lovely Maggie would look," Everett said.

Carolina shot daggers at Maggie. How dare that simple country bumpkin win another cat fight. Well, the battle lines were drawn and she'd not lose the war. Before the whole matter was said and done she would be Mrs. Everett Dulanis and they'd be living right in the middle of the biggest city in the whole United States of America. And that red-haired piece of trash would be back in the sticks where she belonged.

"Come on, *cher,* we must mingle amongst the rest of the guests or else Eulalie will be dressing me down for that." Everett took the empty punch cup from Maggie's hand and put it on a tray as a waiter passed close by them. "Good evening to you two. Enjoy yourselves."

"You will attend the wedding?" Gatlin pressed one more question on Everett.

"Oh, we'll be back in Dodsworth by then," Maggie said. "Everyone is already moaning and groaning about Dr. Everett being gone at all during the cold months. He is needed so badly in the Territory. We do hate to be gone long."

The look in Gatlin's eyes reminded Maggie of a little boy standing outside the store staring in through the screen door at the candy jar. He'd never know the satisfaction of truly being needed. He was just a puppet on Carolina's strings and the strings weren't too sturdy.

"Now what was that cat fight about? I could tell from across the room that Carolina was being somewhat ungracious," Everett said.

"It was nothing." Maggie smiled up at him. "I was just telling her how pretty she looks in all that red. I could never wear that color."

"Thank goodness." Everett's dimple sunk farther than it ever had. "You look just fine in your greens and that dusty pink. I think all women should burn those horrible bustles and go back to wearing simple dresses like you have on. Sitting is easier, and they are so much more attractive."

"Well, thank you again, Everett," Maggie said.

Jefferson was suddenly at Everett's elbow. "I'm sorry to be the bearer of bad news at this festive time, but there is something that requires your immediate attention. A messenger at the front door."

Maggie followed uninvited to the door, cold chills chasing up her spine. Had something dreadful happened to her mother or father? Or Grace? Everett found a cold telegram carrier waiting for him just inside the front door. The man handed him the note, took a generous tip from Everett, and disappeared out the door.

Everett turned the note over and read the same thing Jefferson had just moments before. His overseer was seriously ill. His family had taken him to Baton Rouge for doctoring, and Everett was needed immediately at the sugar plantation. "Oh, no. I'll have to miss Christmas with Eulalie," he said, then felt horrid for his words. Poor Henry was ill and he was worrying about his own pleasures.

"Perhaps it is fate," Maggie said, her voice scarcely a whisper. "The divorce papers went to Louisiana, and we follow them. We can sign them there and it will finally be over for you, Everett."

"I suppose so," he said. "We'll leave as soon as you can get your things packed. We can perhaps catch the midnight train out of Atlanta into New Orleans if we hurry."

"Why New Orleans. I thought you said they'd taken him to Baton Rouge?" she asked.

"They did, but we can get to the plantation faster by going all the way to New Orleans and then taking a stage-coach to Terrebonne County. I'll send a telegram to the plantation for someone to meet us and take us home from there," he explained as they went up the stairs together.

Eulalie winked at Jefferson, who smiled back at her. That woman with all her wiles would keep him on his toes until his dying day. He only hoped her meddling proved to be profitable. He liked Maggie with her honest, forthright attitude. So much like his own daughter Emma's spirit. And he hoped Everett never found out how hard Eulalie had worked to make him open his eyes to what was as plain as a snout on a hog's nose.

Chapter Thirteen

On Christmas morning, when they should have been enjoying all the children around the decorated tree, they were in a stage coach rumbling over a bumpy road toward the southern part of Louisiana. Maggie snuggled under the blanket in the corner of the coach seat. The driver kept the horses going at a steady pace and Everett assured her that they would be at the plantation by supper time. He said at least they would have one decent meal in celebration of the holiday.

Maggie didn't care about a decent meal. She just worried about putting her name on that line when she got to the plantation. It wouldn't be long before James and Elenor brought the papers. Elenor would then know it had all been a sham. Maggie pondered over that idea and found that Elenor or her parents, heck, even the whole town of Dodsworth knowing, didn't bother her anymore. What did upset her was the fact that she was in love with Everett. He didn't laugh often but when he did her heart soared all the way to the clouds. He danced the citified dances well enough and even if he never went to a barn dance with her and learned those steps, she could live with that too.

She'd toyed with the idea of just spitting it out. Telling him how she felt but he'd feel obligated then and she couldn't bear him staying married to her when he didn't love her like she did him. A poet she'd read in one of Violet's books said something about loving something so much you had to let it go. That's the way she loved Everett. Enough to sign the papers and give him his freedom. Even if it tore her heart apart.

"You've been a good sport, Maggie," Everett said, breaking two hours of silence.

"Why wouldn't I be? This has been the adventure of a lifetime, Everett. First a train trip. Then the parties and pretty dresses. Then another train trip and now a real stage coach ride. I know it's a bothersome thing for you but the trip has been wonderful. I'd do it all again. I'm just almighty sorry you missed your holiday with your family." She gazed out the window as she talked, unable to look at him and actually see the disappointment in those brown eyes.

"I'm glad you have that attitude. It'll all be over soon, I promise. Have you decided where you are going?" He asked.

"No. I thought about Atlanta. Eulalie offered to let me help with the boys. Then I thought about one of the towns we've been through on this trip. I just don't know, Everett. It all bewilders me, I have to admit," she said.

"You don't have to decide right now. Matter of fact, you could stay at the sugar plantation if you want to. I seldom ever go there. Only a few times a year to oversee things usually," he said. If only he could open his heart and tell her he'd fallen desperately in love with her. But knowing Maggie, she'd stay married to him and be miserable the rest of her life.

"Thank you. I guess I don't have to make up my mind right now then?" She asked.

"Not at all," he answered and they were silent again.

The sun was straight up in the sky when the driver brought the coach to an abrupt halt, sending Maggie sliding into Everett's lap. He chuckled as he caught her and held her close until everything stopped moving.

"Wonder what's going on?" he said but he didn't push her away.

"Okay, out!" A strange voice said.

"Must have busted a wheel or something," Everett mumbled as he slung open the door to find a shotgun barely inches from his face.

Maggie reached out and pushed the gun aside. "Put that thing away before you hurt someone," she ordered as she stepped out in the cold wind and faced three men. All wearing bandannas over their faces. All brandishing shotguns. Evil pouring out of their eyes.

"You shut your mouth woman. This is a stage robbery not a game. Okay, driver, unload that payroll you got up there," he said.

"Don't have no payroll," the man said fearfully, his hands in the air.

"This is a passenger coach," Everett said as he stepped out of the coach. "I commissioned it special. It isn't carrying anything but my wife and our few belongings."

"Nope, you lie." One man poked him in the chest with the gun. "This stage has a load of gold. Our sources ain't wrong. I think we'll take this woman with us, too."

Everett's heart dropped. Maggie was in danger. Maggie at the ruthless hands of bandits. A thousand thoughts flooded his mind but he couldn't get a handle on any one of them. All he could think about was keeping Maggie safe.

"You may have everything we have, including the coach, but please, just leave us alone," he said.

"Tie him up," the leader said to one of the others. "Pops, you keep your gun trained on that driver. If he moves a muscle, shoot to kill. We'll tie this dandy up and leave him right here. We'll take the woman with us. Ain't had a woman to cook and keep us company since Maria got a bee in her bonnet and went running back to Texas."

"Please, leave my wife alone," Everett stepped back from

the man who'd stood his shotgun beside the stage and grabbed a rope from the saddle of his horse. "I'll pay you to just go away. I'll give you a draft on my bank in Terrebonne County."

All three of them laughed. Maggie's red haired temper got the best of her better judgment. Her husband wasn't trying to be one bit funny. Not when he was pleading for her life and offering them money.

"I'm not going anywhere with you and you're not tying up my husband and leaving him here in this forsaken place." She bowed up to the man with the rope in his hands. Her back was to the other two men and she was so close to the man with the rope that he didn't notice her right hand fumbling in her drawstring reticule.

Suddenly Maggie had a pistol gouged into his ribs. "Now, you tell them to drop the guns or I'll make a bloody hole through your nasty heart," she said.

"Maggie!" Everett exclaimed. "Give me that gun."

"No, sir it's too dangerous," she said. "Might something happen whilst I was handing it to you. No, Everett, you get the rope and start with this varmint. Tie him up real good. Matter of fact, I want him tied to that tree right over there. You going to tell them to drop their guns?"

"No, I'm not. You can shoot me, but they'll take all three of you out and take this stage with the money. I might be dead but so will you," he grinned, showing off tobacco-stained teeth.

"Okay, but I think I'm a good enough shot to take out two of you before I take a slug from that shotgun," she said calmly. "I was the second best shot in all of Nebraska. The only one who bested me was Daddy and he's been at it a little longer. I reckon I can shoot you, spin around and put my next bullet in that fellow with the blue eyes. Might even take out the other one and the rattlesnake right behind him on the flat rock before he can shoot. I'm pretty fast."

"You're lying," the man said.

Maggie really had seen a snake on the rock behind the

man. It didn't look like a rattler so she wondered just exactly why a snake would be out at this time of year. She guessed she'd have to make a believer out of the fool. This whole episode probably meant they wouldn't get a hot supper after all. That fired her temper up even more. She'd looked forward to a long, hot bath and sitting up to a table with Everett one more time before they had to sign those cursed papers.

Well, some things just took proving and this appeared to be one of them. She spun around, shot the eyes out of the snake on the rock between the two men, and had the gun back in the man's gut faster than a gnat can blink. Everett almost swallowed his tongue. He yanked the rope out of the stunned man's hands in the split second Maggie took the gun from his ribs.

"Now, tell them to put their guns on the ground. I've got five more bullets. I keep every chamber loaded and there's only three of you. So, that's one for you and two a piece for your friends. My supper is getting cold and I'm tired of this game," she said, pulling back the trigger to the revolver.

"She's serious," the man said, nodding at his friends, who promptly laid their guns on the ground.

"On your faces, flat down in the dirt, and don't you even look up." She said without taking her eyes from the robber's face. A lot could be determined from staring a man right in the eyes. A flicker here could mean he was up to no good and her finger was itching to pull the trigger already. Lousy, low down thieves anyway.

"Everett, you and the driver tie them up to one of those trees. One tree a piece and make them hug it like a brother. They'll get to know that tree real good by the time we get to the next town and send a posse out here for their sorry hides. Take their shoes off. Socks, too. We'll tie them to the saddle horns on their horses and the sheriff can bring them back with him. Be a long, cold walk if they was to get freed up somehow," she said. She didn't take the gun from the man's side until both the other bandits were secured. Then, turning him over to Everett and the driver, she promptly put her gun away, gathered up the three shotguns, and got back inside the coach.

"Ma'am, I'd hire you on the spot to ride shotgun for me." The driver poked his head in the window and smiled.

"Just protecting what's mine," Maggie muttered but Everett didn't hear it. She knew it would only be hers for a little while longer.

"Where did you learn to shoot like that?" Everett said, amazement written all over his face once the stage was on its way.

"Daddy taught me. I was supposed to be the boy since the first born wasn't. Daddy said I was a natural," she said, wrapping her new black velvet cloak around her to keep out the cold.

"I guess so, but you never mentioned you even had a gun. I sure didn't know you carried one in your reticule," he said.

"Always have. Especially since that business with Violet being kidnapped on her wedding day. Used to leave it at home some. It makes a heavy bag to tote around. I wished I had it on the day Daddy made you marry up with me. I could've, maybe, held him off long enough for you to get away and he cooled down. But I didn't. I figured I'd better be prepared when you said we was going on a stage coach," she said. *Oh, no,* she thought, *here I've really ruined it now. He wants a simpering, little southern lady, like Carolina, who faints at the sight of a mouse. He surely isn't interested in a hog right out of a wallow, toting a six-gun, and shooting the eyes out of snakes.*

"Well, I'm glad you were prepared. I usually have a small hand gun strapped to my leg when I travel but I was in such a hurry, I didn't think about it until we were gone," he said.

"I always wanted one of them kind," she said with a curt nod. "Daddy said I couldn't have one though. By the time a woman got her skirt tails lifted and found it amongst the petticoats, she'd already be in more trouble than she could shoot her way out of. But, if you'd a had one you could have come right out of the stage with it, and . . ." she stammered for words.

"And kept you from danger." He threw back his head and roared. "Maggie, my *jolie fille,* you just saved all our lives. Thank you, *cher.*" He reached across the seat and picked up the hand that had held the gun, bringing it to his lips for a kiss like a true gentleman. "My pride shall not be offended when my hide is intact."

"Good," she smiled brightly. "Momma warned me not to be a show off just cause I can shoot straight and fast. I guess I was a little bit back there, but I wanted those shotguns on the ground. Which, by the way, do I get to keep them since I brought them with me?"

"*Cher,* if the sheriff in the next town wants them for evidence, then I shall buy you three just like them. Why would you want a shotgun when you've got that pistol?"

"Daddy's old blunderbuss isn't working. I just thought maybe I'd send him these three along with a letter and tell him what happened. He'd get a kick out of it," she said.

"Next week three shotguns will be delivered to your daddy. Either these or new ones. You write the letter and tell him all about it. I bet he laughs so hard he cries," Everett kept her hand in his. It wasn't shaking or trembling. Now here was a woman to ride the river with. If only she loved him.

"He'll laugh, but Momma will sure dress me down but good because I left them three out there. She'd a thought we should make them run along behind the stage and take them to the sheriff, but that would slow us down. I wanted you to get home where you could at least have a decent meal on the holiday," she said.

"Maggie, you continue to amaze me," he said, finally letting go of her hand.

"I'm just doing what all women would do in that case,"

she said. "Look at that, Everett! Is that a swamp? Mercy, and this close by. We could have fed them to the alligators. Will I get to see a real alligator?"

"I promise you will if we have to take out the *pirogue* down the Bayou Penchant before I leave," he promised.

"The what down the where?" She wrinkled her forehead.

Every nuance of Maggie was now delightful. He couldn't imagine ever thinking her simple minded or dull. "A *pirogue* is a flat bottomed boat. The Bayou Penchant isn't far from our plantation. James and I played on it when we were children. Fished there quite often in the spring."

"Another adventure," she said, her eyes dancing with excitement. *Another memory,* she thought.

The house on Sweet Penchant was set a quarter mile back down a tree lined lane. Maggie would have liked it to be spring when all the trees were decked out in mint green leaves, but it wasn't and, most likely, she'd never see it at that time of year. Perhaps that was just as well. The stark trees mirrored the reality in her heart. The voice that kept telling her the adventures were over now and they would each go their separate ways.

Maggie's gasp made Everett turn abruptly in the carriage seat. The look on her face wasn't fear but sheer wonder as she stared at the house. A three-story, old, stone-castle-looking edifice that his grandfather built years ago. He'd always taken it for granted. Seeing it through Maggie's eyes was as delightful as riding a train with her.

"Oh, my," she mumbled when he led her to the front door.

It was thrown open by a tall, thin man with silver hair. "Mr. Everett, we are so glad you've arrived. Henry left for a couple of weeks with his wife. We are without a decent cook but at least the cleaning staff is still here. Along with the gardeners and the rest of us."

"No supper," he moaned.

"Where's the kitchen?" Maggie slung her cape from her

shoulders and handed it to the man with the gray hair. "I reckon I'm not going to let either of us starve and I'm hungry."

"This is the new missus?" The man grinned.

"This is Maggie. Maggie, this is our butler and jack-of-all-trades, Robert. He takes care of the organization around here, but he can't boil an egg," Everett handed over his coat and gloves, laughing all the time.

"Well, I can't organize much but I can cook. Have you had supper yet, Robert?" She asked.

"No, ma'am," Robert said.

"Who else hasn't eaten? I'll make enough to feed us a Christmas supper if you'll point me in the direction of the kitchen," Maggie said.

"Well, there's the staff and . . . guess there'd be about ten of us. Most of them have already gone to their own families for the night," Robert said.

Everett continued to grin. Leave it to Maggie. She wouldn't think twice about the hired help sitting at the table with them. "Come on, the kitchen is back here. Have you heard how Henry is? He's not in danger of death is he?"

"No, can't say as he is. His wife just put him in a buggy and they went off. He was fine one day and ailin' the next. She said he was going for help over in Baton Rouge. Said if you was here, where you belonged, you could have cured him up, but she wasn't waiting around and watching Henry die." Robert followed them. Was the new missus really going to cook a meal in that fancy dress? Mercy, but she did have the most unusual looking hair he'd ever seen in all his life. Those eyes were just the color of moss. He'd bet his last dollar that she had a temper to go with it all. Mister Everett Jackson might have just bit off more than he could chew when he married up with that girl. She sure did have more spunk about her than that last bit of blonde fluff he'd brought down here.

An hour later, twelve people sat down at the table which was spread with fried ham, mashed potatoes, gravy, scalloped corn, green beans, fried sweet potatoes, hot biscuits, and even a warm bread pudding with a brown sugar sauce for dessert. Everett sat at one end of the long table and said a simple grace before he began passing the bowls . . . true Oklahoma style, pride etching a brand on his heart. Maggie had the same fortitude of his ancestors who'd carved this sugar plantation out of the unyielding earth. Give her a problem and she'd solve it.

"Mr. Everett, you did good when you married this woman," Robert said, loading his plate for the second time.

"Let me entertain you with a Christmas story," Everett said. He proceeded to tell them the story of Maggie and the bandits, keeping them all in suspense to the end.

"That's a good joke," Robert slapped his knee and laughed. "You had me really believing you right up to the end. But a sweet little lady like that wouldn't be shootin' snakes and tying up stage coach robbers. She can cook almighty good and that's a good story. Now, you two go on and have a bit of Christmas between the two of you. We'll all pitch in and take care of the cleaning duties. We thank you for the supper, Miz Maggie. That's as good a present as we've had all day."

"You are quite welcome," Maggie grinned. So they thought she was a lady. A sweet, little lady at that. Wouldn't they be amazed to know that she was nothing more than a hog straight from the wallow. Dressed up in a fancy dress—maybe. Toting a six gun with one missing bullet—definitely. But what they didn't know wouldn't come back to haunt them when she was gone.

"I'll show you up to your room," Everett took her elbow in his hand and led her up the wide expanse of a staircase.

"This is some house. How can you ever be content in that little cabin in Dodsworth?" She asked.

"It's only for a little while. I've designed a house I intend to build. Bought some land over there in the neighborhood of Ivan Svenson's place. A couple of miles back from your parents' place. It'll be a bit bigger than the cabin but not like this. I don't need two monstrosities to take care of," he chuckled.

"It is beautiful," she said.

"Here's your room. Robert said he was putting us in the master suite, and I didn't have the heart to tell him to just give you Eulalie's old room and let me alone in mine. We'll keep up pretenses a while longer. I don't want to ruin their Christmas. They've wanted me to marry for so long. Sweet Penchant needs an heir, you know."

"I see," she said heavily. "Well, goodnight, then, Everett. I'll have breakfast on the table early so you can get about your business."

"Maggie, you don't have to get up early. You must be tired. I can grab a leftover biscuit from supper which really was delicious, by the way." He stopped at her door.

"Thank you, but I'll be awake. Habit, you know. We'll have our breakfast and then you can take care of things. I'll prowl around if that's all right and get acquainted with this monstrosity," she said.

"That's fine, Maggie. I have an apology to make now, though. I'm sorry," he said bluntly, his conscience pricking his heart so bad it threatened to bleed. "Here it is Christmas, even if it is the end of the day. We have no gifts to open. I should have given it more thought and had something for you."

"Everett, you've given me enough. Adventures. Clothes. Dances. What more could I want? Thank you for all of it, again," she whispered. She tiptoed and kissed him gently on the lips. Yes, the sparks were just like they had been the few times he'd kissed her.

"You really are a wonder," he said. "Goodnight Maggie. Sleep well."

"I'm sure I won't," she said when she was secure behind the bedroom door. She went to the door separating their rooms and slid down it, leaning her face on the smooth oak wood. If only she had the courage to open the door and throw herself into his arms. Just one night of real wedded bliss. One night to sleep curled up in his arms. One morning to wake with his breath on her neck. She could shoot a rattlesnake. She could single-handedly stand off three stage robbers. She could take charge and put a Christmas supper on the table. She could stand her ground when it came to dealing with Carolina Prescott. But, she could no more open that door than she could sprout wings and fly straight to the moon.

Everett had the door knob in his hand. He'd walk through the door, catch her in her camisole and drawers probably and take a royal cussing, but he would tell her that he loved her with his whole heart. That he wanted to tear up the papers James had in his possession over on the next plantation.

All the things were in his heart and in his mind, but he couldn't force himself to turn the knob. Maggie was a remarkable woman. A free spirit with a backbone of steel and a heart of gold. She deserved the man who could make her laugh. The one who could dance the leather off her shoes. He slid down the door and sat on the floor in misery. One oak door separating them. It might as well have been the whole United States of America.

Chapter Fourteen

"What was that noise?" Maggie asked.

"A nutria," Everett said, smiling. "It's like a big swamp rat. Some folks eat them. James and I tried one time but apparently we didn't know how to fix it. Tasted a bit strong and was tougher than shoe leather."

"Sounded like a baby crying or a woman weeping." Maggie shivered.

The fog had lifted but the sun rays were few and far between in the deep shade of the cypress trees dripping with moss the same color as the fog. A water moccasin slithered into the water, but the sight of the snake didn't affect her nearly as much as the plaintive cries of the nutria.

"That's what most folks say when they hear them for the first time," Everett said. "After a while, it's kind of like the grandfather clock in the foyer at Sweet Penchant. You just don't hear it anymore."

"Where are we going?" Maggie asked, dipping her fingertips in the cold water of the bayou.

"Just down to a little island and back. I promised you a ride in a *pirogue* when you held off the bandits. I don't know if we'll see a gator this time of the year, but you can have your ride down the swamps," he said.

Before James and Elenor come for supper and bring the

papers, he thought mournfully. *But we won't talk about that right now. We'll enjoy the quiet ride in the swamp, have lunch on the island, and go home to Sweet Penchant for the signing.* Somehow the whole thing had gotten out of hand and too complicated for Everett to understand. How could he have gone from despising Maggie to loving her in two short months?

"I can't imagine living like this. In a fancy house with people to clean it for you. A cook, a butler, gardeners. And a swamp so close you could lose yourself in it on days when the world got to closing in," Maggie said more to herself than to Everett.

"It's just living, Maggie. Sweet Penchant was left to me when Momma and Papa died with the understanding that Eulalie would have half the profits each year. The actual land and house will be passed onto my son," he explained.

"Then why don't you live here? Doctors are needed everywhere, Everett. This is your inheritance. How can you make your son love it from so far away? He needs to ride in a *pirogue.* He needs to fish in these waters and bring in the sugar crop. The love won't be there if you don't foster it," Maggie said.

"To have a son, one must have a wife. Not many women can handle this kind of life, Maggie. It's demanding," he said.

I could handle it. I could love it, she thought. *I already do. Even if we had to live in one of the tenant cabins, I'd love it. It's the most peaceful place in the whole world. But you couldn't ever love me even if I could produce a dozen sons for you.*

"You're probably right, Maggie. I love it here. It's peaceful and I always hate to leave. But I don't know about living here all the time." He poled the boat around a bend and the island came into view.

"You ought to think about it. Is that our island? Will there be shells on it?" she asked.

"Yes and yes." He smiled. Maggie was fascinated with

the simplest things in life. Shells. A ride in a weathered old *pirogue.* The day after Christmas he'd come in from the back side of the plantation and found her laughing with the maids; all of them up to their elbows in wash tubs as they shared laundry duties. Yesterday she had a pair of pruning shears, carefully nipping the rose bushes. This was the month, she'd explained, to take care of the orange hips if you wanted to grow a few roses from seed.

He poled the pirogue right up to the bank and tied it to a willow stump. "Now, my lady." He held out his hand.

She carefully stood up, fearful that she might rock the boat and fall out into the cold water. She braced herself for the feeling that would rattle her bones when his fingers touched hers. "It is a mite chilly," she said, hoping he attributed the shiver to the weather.

"I've got a blanket to cover you with while we eat our sandwiches," he said, drawing a basket from the boat, along with a couple of thick blankets.

She could scarcely sit still long enough to eat the turkey sandwich; then she was off to explore the island that was scarcely bigger than the church house in Dodsworth. Everett laid back with his head propped against the trunk of a weeping willow tree and watched her in utter amazement. Every shell brought on a whoop of delight. By the time they were ready to leave, she had her faded green dress tail full of them and her mossy green eyes were sparkling. It was simply because it was all new, though. In a year or two she'd be sick of the loneliness and begging to be taken back to Dodsworth where she could go to the barn dances. Where she could laugh with her friends, Emma and Violet, and visit with Duncan at the general store.

"Everett, it's been a perfect day," she declared when he helped her back into the pirogue. "I'm so glad you brought me into the swamp—I'll cherish these shells forever."

"You are quite welcome for the day, Maggie," Everett said.

"A wonderful day, to be topped off by a wonderful

night." She examined her shells one by one as he poled them back toward the plantation.

"Oh?"

"Yes. I haven't seen Elenor since her wedding day," Maggie said.

"I see," Everett said.

Silence surrounded them. The sound of a faraway nutria, the plop of a water moccasin as it slithered into the water from a stump, the *pirogue* gliding through the water, and the breaking of two hearts were the only noises in the whole swamp.

"Elenor!" Maggie threw open the door and her arms at the same time. She met her sister on the porch in a ferocious hug. "Come inside. I've got a pot roast big enough to feed an army in the oven and biscuits all ready to cook. Mercy, I've missed you. I've got to tell you about the island out in the swamp and show you my shells."

"And I've got to tell you about the plantation James and his brothers own right next to this one. I can't believe he'd ever want to set up practice in Dodsworth, but I'm glad he does," Elenor whispered. "This place is all right—but it's not home."

Everett and James knew when they'd been put aside, so the two of them retired to the den where at last James laid the papers on Everett's desk. "Now or later?" James asked.

"Not until after supper. Maybe just before you leave. No need in wrecking Maggie's evening," Everett said, staring out the window at the gray winter sky.

"You haven't told her today is the day?" James asked.

"No, not yet. I promised her a trip into the swamp. I didn't want to spoil it," Everett said.

"My friend, are you sure you want to do this? I think maybe you've actually fallen in love with your wife. Is there no way to make this marriage work? These are just papers, no good unless you both sign them and then they are filed at the courthouse in Atlanta," James said.

"It doesn't matter how I feel. Maggie deserves a very different type man than what I am. Someone who is lively and spirited. She's a free spirit, you know? One in a million. It might have worked if it had started differently, but when two people make vows because of a shotgun, they don't really mean them. Maggie was putting up just as much fight as me that day, James. And she's made it clear several times that she sure doesn't want to be married to me."

"What do you want?" James asked.

"To make Maggie happy," Everett said.

In the kitchen Elenor grabbed one of the cook's aprons and wrapped it around her tiny waist twice, just like Maggie had already done. "I can't wait to get back home, Maggie. By the time we get there, James says our house will be finished and I can buy furniture for it. Real store-bought stuff. Can you believe it? You'll have to be the first one to eat dinner with us in our new house. I'll invite you and Momma and Daddy and Grace and of course, Dr. Everett . . . and maybe Ivan."

Maggie winced. She'd never be there to see Elenor's new house or eat supper with her. She'd never make biscuits or help her sister in the kitchen.

"Ivan?" Maggie finally realized what Elenor had said.

"Yes, just before we left he brought a flower to Grace. I first thought he was coming to pay court to me. I mean, after all, I chased the man ruthlessly for months. I 'bout fainted when I saw him coming up the lane carrying this pot with a big red poinsettia in it that he'd actually bought in Guthrie. I figured I'd have to break his heart and tell him I was going to marry James Beauchamp. But when I opened the door he blushed scarlet as your hair and asked for Grace."

"Oh, my." Maggie giggled. "What did Grace do?"

"She was nice about it, but after he left, she stomped and ranted like only Grace can do. Momma sure enough should have named her anything but Grace the way she lets her temper run rampant when she's mad. Said there wasn't no way she was letting Ivan court her. She didn't like one thing about him. Not his blonde hair or blue eyes or how tall he was, or how his pants were an inch too short and his feet two sizes too big." Elenor laughed.

"Well, guess he wasted his money on a posey," Maggie said. "And you got to remember Momma didn't just name her Grace. She's Grace Benjamin, and she got Daddy's temper along with his name. Not even to mention Momma's temper. I guess old Ivan better go casting his eyes around at some of the other girls in Dodsworth."

"I suppose. But strange things do happen, don't they? Who would have thought you would be married to the doctor or me to James. Way back last summer, I figured I'd settle down with Ivan and you'd be an old maid," Elenor said. "Here we are both married. I love being married, Maggie. It's the most wonderful thing in the whole world, isn't it?"

"I wouldn't know," Maggie said.

"I mean, at night when James holds me close and whispers all those sweet words in my ear . . . what did you just say?" Elenor stopped in her tracks.

"I said I wouldn't know. I didn't want to marry Everett, but Daddy had that six-gun on his hip and I had forgotten my gun. It was crazy of me, since I knew what happened to Violet. I should have remembered to put it in my reticule. Then I could have held Daddy at bay until Everett ran away and Daddy cooled down. Everett sure didn't want to marry me. He said I was as suited to being his wife as a hog right out of a wallow. At first it made me mad but then I figured he was right. Anyway, we planned on getting the whole thing annulled but then we'd stayed together in the cabin and it had to be a divorce. I figure James is in there in the den right now with the papers for us to sign and it will be all over. I'm not going back to Dodsworth, Elenor. I couldn't do that to Everett. He's got a practice there and it might hinder it. So he's going to give me some money and I'm going far away. I haven't decided where yet. I might just stay here for a few months. I love this place better than anywhere I've ever been in my whole life. Then I'll decide where I want to go before he comes back next summer for a week."

"Oh, Maggie, you mean you've never . . ." Elenor wiped away a tear.

"Never. I had the bedroom downstairs in the cabin and Everett took the loft. These plantation houses have got separate bedrooms for wives so it hasn't been a problem. We just keep the door shut." Maggie pulled the biscuits from the oven and set them on the work table.

"I'm so sorry. I didn't know. I thought you were so much in love. I thought I could see it in your eyes. Have you . . ." Elenor could scarcely believe what she'd just heard.

"Have I what?" Maggie kept working, getting dishes out of the cupboard to load with food.

"I could swear you loved him. Do you?" Elenor asked.

"It wouldn't matter if I did. He deserves another kind of wife, Elenor. One kind of like Carolina Prescott. Everett is a special person. He's really smart and I'm not the . . ." Maggie couldn't finish the sentence.

"I'll miss you so bad," Elenor said.

"I'll miss you worse. But like Daddy said, I made my bed that night. Even if I didn't know I was making it, I did, and I have to live with those decisions. We can write long letters. I'll tell you about the plantation and you can keep me up on Dodsworth. Don't you dare forget to write me a long letter when Violet has that baby," Maggie said, attempting to lighten the heaviness surrounding them both. "Now let's the two of us go in there like Listen women. Strong as an ox and mean as a rattlesnake with a sore tooth. I'll sign the papers and get it over with so we don't have to think about it during our supper. Momma would have our hides tacked to the smokehouse door if we didn't act like we was her daughters. Remember she left her whole family in Nebraska and came to the land run with Daddy. We come from strong stock, Elenor, and we won't whine."

"Well, I guess I have to live with it, but I darn sure don't have to like it." Elenor looped her arm in her older sister's.

"Daddy will take you to the smokehouse and tan your hide for using words like that." Maggie smiled, but her pretty green eyes were dull.

"Ladies?" James looked up from the desk where he and Everett read over the divorce decree.

"We'll take care of this business," Maggie said. "And then we'll forget all about it and set up to the table for our supper."

"Are you sure, Maggie?" James asked. It was as plain as the precious turned up nose on his adorable wife's face that Maggie and Everett were both in love and too stubborn to admit it. Signing those papers would be the biggest mistake either of them ever made. He just knew it down in the middle of his bones. Call it "the sight" or plain old Louisiana voo-doo, but it was there. A feeling that kept telling him to grab the papers and tear them to shreds. To tell them both to wake up and see what everyone else was looking at. But he didn't do one thing but wait.

"Are you sure this is the right thing to do, Everett? Maggie just told me all about it," Elenor said. "Maybe if you waited a couple of more months?"

"Maggie?" Everett looked deep into those green eyes he dreamed about at night now. All the way to the bottom of Maggie's soul, he looked, and somewhere he found the only woman he could ever love.

"Where do I sign?" she asked. She'd go first and that would give Everett a chance to back out. If he said he couldn't do it, she'd tear the paper up herself.

"Right here." James pointed to a line and she wrote, *Maggie Listen Dulanis.* The first and only time she'd ever written her married name. The last time she'd ever have occasion to use his name. For just a moment she really was his wife. Long enough to stare at her legal name.

It was done. Over. Finished. So why did she feel like the biggest part of her heart was lying on the paper beside her name?

Everett had hoped against hope that she'd change her mind at the last moment and declare that she couldn't be a divorced woman. If she had, he would have courted her and made her love him. But she'd seemed eager to put her name on the line. So he took the pen from her hand and signed his own name right above hers.

It was done. Over. Finished. At last. So why did he feel like someone had just gut shot him and left him in a swamp to die?

"Now let's go have supper. That was nothing more than taking care of what shouldn't have even begun." She tried to maintain a lighthearted tone for Elenor's sake.

"Did I tell you that Henry is recovered and he and Milly will be returning to Sweet Penchant tomorrow morning?" Everett followed Maggie's lead.

"So when are you leaving?" James asked.

"I'll be going tomorrow afternoon." Everett watched Maggie's face. Was that a tear she brushed away or just a hair in her eyes? "But Maggie has decided to stay on here a while. Until she figures out where she wants to go. I'd thought maybe we wouldn't say anything about the papers for a while. The staff here can just think of Maggie as the Missus a while longer. It might make things easier. So if you two wouldn't tell anyone over in your neck of the woods. . . ."

"No more lies," Maggie said determinedly.

"It's not a lie," James intervened. "It's just not telling everything all at once, Maggie."

More thoughts than she could gather in chased through her mind. To be mistress of Sweet Penchant, even for a little while, was more than she could comprehend. She'd do a good job for Everett. She could take care of things while he was gone and by the time summer came, she'd decide just where the train would take her. Maybe they could even make an agreement that the week he came to Louisiana, she would go to Dodsworth to visit her family and friends. Decisions. Decisions. Thank goodness none of them had to be made right then.

"Okay," she said slowly. "Now Elenor, come and help me put supper on the table. These two men are hungry, I'd dare say, and the biscuits are getting cold."

She wore a faded blue dress and one of Milly's aprons tied around her waist. Her red hair was twisted up haphazardly on the top of her head and there was a smudge of flour on her cheek. Everett wanted to reach out and brush it away, then kiss her one last time, but he just watched her walk out of the room and back to the kitchen.

"Elenor will miss her," James said softly.

"So will I," Everett admitted honestly.

The lady who stared back at Maggie in the mirror had dark circles under her eyes and a haunted look on her face, but there didn't seem to be anything she could do about it. She'd held a cold wash cloth against her face for a long time. That didn't help. She tried smiling, but it came out more like a grimace than a grin. She didn't want Everett to remember her with sadness.

The whole marriage had started out on the wrong foot, but she didn't need to make him feel guilty about the ending. She loved him too much for that. She'd smile and wave and promise to keep Sweet Penchant in order until he returned. She got a little color in her cheeks by pinching them, but it faded fast.

She could hear him in the other room, making ready to leave. The carriage waited. Henry had arrived that morning, looking hale and hearty. Milly, a short, stout little lady with gray streaks in her dark hair, fussed and fretted in her kitchen. She'd slammed pots and pans around and made so much noise, Maggie had finally asked her just what she was angry about.

"I go away for two weeks. Put up with ornery grandchildren in a little bitty house, all for nothing. Miss Eulalie said it would work—but it didn't. I come back and we still don't have what Sweet Penchant craves," Milly talked in circles. "It's not you, my *cher*. The staff says you are the right one. Some folks are just blind and you can't scrape the scales from their eyes. I am disappointed. That is all."

"I still don't understand but maybe I will later," Maggie had said. Later, she pondered over the words and understood even less than she did before she escaped to the safety of her bedroom.

The door to Everett's room shut softly, and she heard his footsteps going down the stairs. She inhaled deeply. This was it. The time had come. He would go and she would stay. They were no longer bound by shotgun vows. She stepped out into the hallway and followed him down the steps.

"Stay as long as you want," he said stiffly on the front porch.

"Thank you . . . for all of it," she said.

"Maggie?" He turned quickly to tell her he loved her but couldn't make himself say the words.

She reached out and hugged him tightly. Even if they weren't married, she'd lived with this man for many weeks. They'd had adventures together. Shared lives, even if not the marriage bed. A hug seemed the least she could do in way of thanks.

He tilted her head back and kissed her. One more time. One last time. Because he'd never see his sweet Maggie again. He was sure of it. She'd go on to find happiness with some other man. For some reason, her lips tasted faintly salty. She kissed him back, savoring every emotion rippling through her body and soul. It was the last time she'd ever feel his heart beat next to her breast. The last time she'd feel his mouth on hers. She would enjoy it and remember it forever.

"You take care of yourself," he said hoarsely.

"You be careful. You got your gun on your leg?" she asked stiffly.

"I got it. You keep yours in your reticule, *cher.*" He tried to force a smile but couldn't.

"I will. Good-bye, Everett." She stepped back and waved as he got into the carriage.

"Good-bye, Maggie," he said and tilted his head so he could keep her in his sight as long as possible.

When there was nothing more to see, not even a faint dot, nothing more to hear, not even the slightest whisper of a wagon wheel leaving Sweet Penchant, Maggie slowly went back upstairs to her bedroom. She opened the door separating her world from Everett's and went into the master bedroom. She laid on his bed, inhaled the smell of him from the pillow where he had lain his head the night before, and gave way to all the emotions she'd kept bottled up from the time she'd stood in front of Preacher Elgin and promised to love Everett Dulanis, until she'd signed the divorce papers just yesterday.

Maggie wept.

Chapter Fifteen

Everett awoke to the squeals of two little boys in the nursery. His heart ached for children of his own. A son for Sweet Penchant like Maggie said. He'd left a week ago that day. Days and days of endless hours, he had spent walking through the fields trying to find peace. It wasn't his to be had; and he'd realized late last night before he finally went to sleep that though he was in Atlanta, his heart wasn't there. And it wouldn't be in Dodsworth, either. It was back in Louisiana, and a body and soul could not survive when it was divided.

The time had come when he could put it off no longer. He had to file the papers so he could get on with life. Even if life without Maggie wasn't life at all. He'd ride into town and make himself take care of the business that very morning. It would be done then and he could go on back to Dodsworth to his practice, even if he didn't want to be there. At least it was where his work was, and that would keep him busy.

He had to go back. The folks there had put their trust in him. Violet was expecting a baby and he had to deliver it. Little Alford would get into something else and need more stitches or fall out of a tree and need his arm set. He was needed in Dodsworth. Trouble was, his heart wasn't there anymore. A simple girl with the strangest red hair had stolen it and now held it captive on his very own plantation in Louisiana. He couldn't go back there. He loved her too much to tie her wings and harness her free spirit. Maggie was born to ride trains and gather shells. Not live a humdrum life of a doctor and plantation owner's wife.

He swallowed a cup of coffee in the kitchen but bypassed breakfast. He avoided his sister as well as Jefferson. They'd both given him a wide berth while he tried to work through his emotions this past week, but he didn't want to tell them that today he really was going to file the papers. Today he was going to go into the courthouse and actually do the deed instead of standing on the steps like he'd done every day that week. And tomorrow morning, he was going back to a cold cabin in Dodsworth with nothing but a little gray kitten to keep him company.

The cold winter wind whipped at Everett's top coat as he made his way to the courthouse. All that was left was filing the papers and the past two months would be erased. He hoped that by paying his fee and filing the papers it would erase the whole episode from his heart as well.

"Everett, what are you doing out on a bitter cold morning like this?" A voice stopped him in front of a hotel. He looked up to find Gatlin getting out of a buggy right beside him. That's all he needed right now: to run into Gatlin and have to listen to all the wedding plans and how wonderful Carolina was.

"Just a little business to take care of before I go to Oklahoma," Everett said. "Good to see you old man, but I must be on my way. Give my best to Carolina and have a happy honeymoon."

"Would you please put off your business for a half an hour, my man? Come inside to the lobby and have a cup of coffee with me. Take the chill off. It'll be our last time to visit for a long time if you're going back to the wilderness. And I need to talk to you so badly," Gatlin said.

Gatlin was the last person in the world Everett wanted

to listen to right then. Gatlin who'd taken Carolina away from him. Gatlin who'd betrayed their friendship. "I really shouldn't. I'm on a tight schedule. Got a train to catch first thing tomorrow morning and I promised my sister the afternoon with her and the twins," Everett lied and crossed his fingers behind his back like he'd done when he and James were small boys.

"I need to talk," Gatlin said seriously. "It's important. Please, Everett."

There didn't seem to be any way out of it. Even though Gatlin wasn't as old a friend as James was, he was a close friend. At least until the business with Carolina. Everett nodded and followed him inside to the restaurant located in the lobby of the biggest hotel in Atlanta. A waiter found them a table in a far corner, and Gatlin ordered two cups of coffee. "I don't know how to say this, Everett. I owe you an apology, to begin with."

Everett held up his hand. "It's not necessary, Gatlin. I truly wish you and Carolina all the happiness in the world."

"That's the problem. Happiness and Carolina do not go together, Everett. I've been in Atlanta for a month now. The most miserable month of my whole life. She's not the woman I fell in love with. But then I wonder if she was ever that woman. I think I invented a personality to go with her beauty." Gatlin sipped his coffee.

Everett looked at his easy-going, fun-loving friend and noticed for the first time that his face was drawn; his eyes set in dark circles; his smile gone.

"I'm so sorry," Everett said honestly.

"What am I to do?" Gatlin pleaded. "I've given my pledge. The wedding is scheduled in less than a week and I feel like a cornered rat. To tell the truth, I'm jealous as all get out of you right now. Maggie isn't only beautiful on the outside but on the inside as well. Lord, she's exactly what I thought Carolina was. I'm afraid I've stolen the wrong woman from my best friend. I should have stolen his wife, not his fiancée." Gatlin tried an attempt at humor but it fell between them like a brick.

Everett smiled wanly. "I don't really think you would have had much luck there. Maggie has a mind of her own. And besides, I didn't exactly choose her for my wife. Why don't you call the whole wedding off and go home to Dodsworth with me?" Everett offered.

"Her father would send a posse to shoot me. There would be dead or alive posters on every fence post between here and there." Gatlin laughed hollowly.

An idea was born in the next sip of coffee. It was so farfetched, though, that Everett hesitated to even put it into words. It would never work. Not in a million years. Not even in Indian Territory. But then it might. He worried it around in his mind like a dog with a bone for a few minutes.

"What's going on in your mind, my friend? I've seen that look before. Remember we went through college and med school together," Gatlin asked, hoping against all hope that Everett could find some light in a dark, dark world.

"It's a long shot," Everett said.

"It's better than what I've got right now, which is a noose of misery tightening around my neck every second," Gatlin said seriously.

"Well, here it is. Carolina came to Dodsworth to see me. Actually, to tell me that she'd decided to marry you. She hated it there. I mean absolutely hated it, Gatlin. So if you suddenly felt a calling to go and practice medicine among the poor folks who need your services so much more than the upper crust of Georgia's finest . . ." Everett let the idea soak in for a moment.

"Then she'd throw a fit. I mean a real fit. She'd stomp and rave and throw vases and china, Everett. She absolutely abhorred that place. Oh, I see . . ." Gatlin's face lit up in a brilliant smile. "But she said the town was tiny. It surely could not support two doctors and you've already got a shingle hung out."

"It don't take much to change a shingle, does it. Matter of fact, I bet Emma and Jed would call up the sign maker and have one done for you just to get a doctor in Dodsworth. Not to mention Violet and Orrin. They actually built the clinic there on Main Street for me."

"You're losing me," Gatlin said.

"I'm giving you my practice. I can't leave the good people of Dodsworth without a doctor. They need one too badly. Tell Carolina that you ran into me on the streets this morning and I was worried about this very thing. Tell her you felt the place calling you. That we'd always talked about working in a small town and this is the opportunity of a lifetime. Then tell her that you made the decision without talking to her because you are aware of how much she loves you. That you have no doubt she'd share a tent on the side of a raging river just to get to be your wife. Then simply say you are taking her and moving to Oklahoma the day after the wedding. There's a small two-room cabin that Emma and Jed own that I'm sure the both of you will be very happy in. A little honeymoon cottage. Praise it up and tell her that you know she'll be happy there because that's where your heart has always been. You realize she couldn't live there with me because she didn't love me that much, but she does you. Tell her that you know she will remember the cabin because that's where Maggie and I lived," Everett said, his heart lighter than it had been in a week.

"I've always wanted to practice in a small town with common folks who need me," Gatlin said wistfully.

"So?" Everett held his breath.

"What are you going to do, then? If I take your practice? What if the people there don't like me as well as they did you? I don't have the finances of a plantation to fall back on if I don't make it in the world of medicine," Gatlin said.

"They will love you. Just take a word of advice. You'll be going to spring dances. Be sure you don't offer to take a lonely damsel in distress home if she gets left in a storm," Everett said with a chuckle.

"I heard that's what happened to you and Maggie. I'll not be looking for a wife, Everett. This time has brought me to my senses. Besides, you've already gotten the cream of the whole crop. She's a real find, Everett, and you are a lucky, lucky man," Gatlin said.

"I know, my friend, I know." Everett carefully avoided the other question. The one about what was he going to do if he didn't return to Dodsworth. He had to worry that over in his mind for a little while longer before he actually put the plans into motion.

"I'm going to do it. Right now. I'm going to demand an audience with Carolina. If you see a storm to the east of the city and a big ball of flames exploding you'll know what it's all about. Thank you, Everett. You've been getting me out of trouble for so long I don't know how I'd manage without you." Gatlin stood up and extended his hand.

Everett took it with a smile. Fate, strange as it was, had just opened his eyes. He should have been married to Carolina himself right at that moment. She didn't love Gatlin, or she wouldn't have thrown herself at Everett at the Christmas party. Gatlin would make a fine country doctor and Dodsworth would love him, maybe even more than they had loved Everett. He wouldn't tell him about Ben Listen's shotgun being empty. Not today. Besides, Ivan might have already married Grace by the time Gatlin got to Dodsworth. And there was that pretty little school teacher coming right after the holiday vacation. Everett had sat on the committee that hired her. She might be just the ticket for Gatlin.

"So what do I do when I get there?" Gatlin asked when they were back out in the cold.

"Nothing. Emma and Jed have already gone home. I'll send a telegram to them to pick you up at the train station instead of me. Here, take this ticket. I won't be using it now." Everett pulled the ticket he'd just bought an hour before from his vest pocket. "Pack your clothing and take your black bag. The rest is there waiting for you. There's a buggy in the barn at their place, a horse to pull it with, and a small bank account in Guthrie that the practice has accumulated in the past few months. Brand, spanking new equipment in the clinic. Lots of pregnant women in the county. Sometimes they pay in chickens and apples, but the right woman can even take care of that kind of thing."

"But you've already got Maggie." Gatlin managed a weak smile. "And besides, I'm through with taking that which does not belong to me. Matter of fact, I may be a self-proclaimed bachelor for the rest of my days. I'll learn to pluck my own chicken and peel my own apples. Everett, I can't thank you enough for all this."

"Gatlin, it's me who should be thanking you." Everett clapped a hand on his friend's shoulder. "I was as close to stepping into misery as you are. Looking back, I wonder if that's why I didn't go to Dodsworth to begin with. I knew she'd hate it there; and it was a test. Did she love me enough to put her own selfishness aside? I got my answer when you were able to sway that love. Now you have yours. Carolina Prescott may never love anyone half as much as she does her own self, and we'll not let her ruin our friendship. Just grab this chance and go with it. Write me a long letter when you get there."

"I'm so glad I saw you walking on the street, Everett," Gatlin said. "Where will I send the letter? To Crooked Oaks?"

"No, send it to Sweet Penchant. I'm going home, Gatlin. Home where I belong," Everett said.

Chapter Sixteen

The trees were minty green with new growth, and a descendent of Patches had a brand new litter of kittens in the basket beside the fireplace. Everett propped his bare feet on the footstool in front of the rocking chair. His hair had gray streaks now, and there were wrinkles around the dimple in his chin. Maggie opened the bedroom door and he patted his lap like he did every morning. She curled up in her favorite place and listened to his heart beat. Their children were growing up happy in Sweet Penchant. Peace surrounded her like a shroud and she didn't want to ever open the door to the world. She and Everett could stay right there on the plantation until the undertaker came to take them both to the graveyard. Or they could go back to living in a two-room cabin with a loft. It didn't matter where Maggie lived, as long as Everett was there to grow old with her.

There was a brief moment when she knew she was dreaming again and she fought the real world, wanting so badly to remain asleep just a little longer. She shut her eyes tightly, not wanting to see the light of day. "Please," she whispered a prayer. "I don't want to wake up. I want to stay asleep and grow old with Everett."

Her prayers weren't answered.

A brilliant winter sunrise lit up his bedroom where she'd

taken to sleeping since he left more than a week ago. She drew his dressing robe around her slim frame and walked out onto the balcony. The cold winter air made her shiver, making her remember the effect his kisses had on her. How could she have ever let him go without speaking her mind?

She needed a cup of coffee. Strong, black coffee like Milly made every morning. She slipped a pair of Everett's socks on her feet and padded down to the kitchen where Milly was already bustling around. The aroma of frying bacon and coffee permeating the air made Maggie's stomach growl.

"So you are up and around," Milly said. "In his robe and socks again. I swear I never saw anyone love someone else the way you do that man. Why didn't you just go back to Oklahoma with him? You shouldn't be here—even though we will all cry when you go. You should both be here. Making pretty red-haired boys to take care of the sugar crops. My husband will not live forever, you know."

"Milly!" Maggie almost dropped her coffee cup.

"Well, it is the truth, *cher.* Eulalie was sure it would work. But it didn't. So now I have waited a week to ask. Why didn't it work?" Milly asked.

"What?" Maggie was used to Milly's constant chatter, but she was surely talking in circles and riddles this morning.

"Eulalie wrote a letter to us. Special. Delivered by a man on a horse she'd paid to bring it right to our hands. She said Everett Jackson didn't know he was in love with you and she was sending both of you here for some time alone. She said if you had to be together without everyone else interfering, both of you would figure out that you were in love and stay married. She said you loved him but he was a stubborn Cajun. So we played like my husband was sick and we went away for a little while. Only it didn't work," Milly snapped.

Maggie giggled. So that's what had Milly in a stew. "Eulalie was just seeing what she wanted to see. Our hearts can't see so we have to depend on our eyes. Eulalie is like you folks here at Sweet Penchant. She wants to see Everett happy. Married and with children to inherit this great place. So her heart said he loved me and she wanted it to be so. I'm sorry it isn't," she said.

Milly stopped stirring gravy and stared at Maggie, beautiful even in a man's oversized dressing robe, with her hair stringing down her back so far she had to flip it over her shoulder to keep from sitting on it. The girl had no idea of her own worth and beauty, or that Everett was in love with her. "Well, *cher,* my heart tells me the same thing. Me, I think you are both two stubborn people. Like little children. I won't show you my toy until you show me yours."

"Milly!" Maggie exclaimed.

"Me, I call it like this Cajun sees it," she said, and went back to her cooking.

Maggie carried her coffee out the back door to the barren rose garden. In the spring it would be beautiful; she looked forward to seeing it there in all its many colored splendor. She'd plant her new ones in that corner and water them diligently. But that was only if . . .

"Maggie, where are you?" Elenor called from the door. "Come inside. I've come to tell you good-bye."

She reluctantly pulled the robe around her flannel nightgown and went back into the house. There had been an idea forming in her mind. Was it something about the roses or Everett? She'd set her cup down and something came to her, but then it was gone before it ever actually reached its destination.

"Good grief, you look horrid," Elenor said laughing.

"Well, you look gorgeous." Maggie grinned. Elenor wore her traveling dress the seamstresses had made in Atlanta. A dark blue serge with a matching fur-lined cape. Her blonde hair glistened against the soft light brown collar.

"Are you just going to sit down here in this place and become a crazy old woman?" Elenor scolded, ushering her upstairs. "You're going to get dressed and come to supper over at our place. I won't take no for an answer. I can spend the morning here but I've got a million things to do before we leave tomorrow. Now, the pink velvet?" Elenor threw open the wardrobe door.

"No." Maggie plopped down on the bed. The door into Everett's room was still open. Odd. He had to be gone before she could open the door. Kind of like his heart. Not until he was gone did she begin to realize what she'd seen inside his soul that evening they'd signed the papers. He probably didn't even know it himself. That he did care about her. About plain old simple Maggie.

"Then the green?" Elenor asked.

"No. I'm not going to dinner with you. We'll have the morning and then you can go on back to Atlanta. Or you can help me pack. I've decided what I'm going to do after all," Maggie said.

Tears filled Elenor's eyes. "Where?"

"I'm not sure just where. I've got a couple of things to see about, but I think I know what I want now. It just might take a little spell to get it." Maggie drew her eyebrows down into a solid line across her eyes.

"Okay, Maggie, just tell me straight out what you're thinking." Elenor sat down on the bed beside her. "It's got something to do with Everett, doesn't it?"

"Why do you say that?"

"You're wearing his robe and his socks, which are ten miles too long for your little feet. And the door is open to his room, which means you probably spend a lot of time in there. You ain't foolin' me. You are in love with him. James swears he loves you, too, but that he thinks he's not the right man for you," Elenor said.

"He's probably not," Maggie said. "He's sure not what I wanted. But my heart seems to think it knows better than me."

"Well, I thought I wanted Ivan Svenson," Elenor giggled. "But my heart sure told me different the first time I laid eyes on James Beauchamp. It pert near jumped right out of my chest. So our minds and our hearts do have different ideas, that's for sure."

"That's right," Maggie said.

"So where are you going first?" Elenor asked.

"To Dodsworth, to have it out with Everett," Maggie said. "I'm going to catch a coach to New Orleans and a train to Dodsworth."

"You can go as far as Shrieveport with us," Elenor said excitedly. "We can all leave together in the morning."

"No, I'm leaving this afternoon. Should be in New Orleans by daybreak and on the first train headed north. If things don't work out for us after all, then I'm comin' right back down here. I love this place, Elenor. I may just be that crazy old woman you mentioned. Living in his robes and wearing his socks. Anything to be close to him," Maggie whispered. "But I've got to go home and speak my mind. Momma would have my hide if she'd known I didn't speak my mind. She trained us up to do that, you know. We ain't simpering, spineless women. We got ideas and a mind."

"And if you don't speak up how's a body to know what you're thinkin'," they said in unison in the very tone their mother used.

"Here, I'll help you pack," Elenor said. "Who knows? You might be getting remarried by the time I get back to Dodsworth! That's something, though. Married when you didn't want to be. Divorced—and now going home to chase your husband. Funny world, ain't it?"

"Yes, it is," Maggie said, folding the robe to put in her trunk.

The gun was heavy in her velvet drawstring reticule that sorely mismatched her old gray wool coat and her faded green calico dress. She watched the barren countryside speed past the coach window by moonlight. No bandits stopped them, but she didn't sleep a wink all night long.

She marched up to the ticket window in the train station

and asked to purchase fare to Guthrie, Oklahoma. The man behind the window eyed her up and down several times before he told her how much that would cost. He expected her to burst into tears and walk away, but she pulled out several bills and asked if there would be an extra charge for a porter to put her luggage in the sleeper.

"No, ma'am," he said, perking right up. She was most likely one of those people the train bosses sent to see how courteous the employees were. "I'll see to it they are in your sleeper by the time you board. And you have a nice day, ma'am."

"Thank you." She almost laughed. Money sure did have a loud voice didn't it?

She laid her coat on the bottom bunk when she reached her tiny little room. She'd sleep on the top bunk as soon as the train got underway. Her eyes were heavy, telling her she needed rest. By nightfall they'd be in Shrieveport and she'd have to change trains there. According to her ticket, she'd have a two-hour layover.

She unpacked Everett's robe from the trunk and used it to cover with as she laid down and shut her eyes. It was a long way to Guthrie, Indian Territory, but that's where her heart was. With Everett. She'd tell him exactly how she felt when she got there. And if he didn't feel the same way? Well, then she'd face that when the time came. At least she'd know for sure if Eulalie, Elenor, and Milly were all seeing what they wanted to see instead of the real truth.

What did Maggie want? she asked herself as she slipped into slumber.

Maggie wanted Everett to think she was more than a hog out of a wallow.

Maggie wanted Everett to kiss her again.

Maggie wanted Everett to love her.

Chapter Seventeen

Everett had slept very little during the trip. His nerves were on edge worse than they'd ever been. Nothing—not life, not medical school—had prepared him for the feeling of hopelessness as he waited for the train to reach its destination. No wonder the word *love* had four letters and not five or three. It was evenly divided. Two for one heart and two for the other. Unless they were joined, it wasn't complete.

The first leg of the journey over, Everett had a three hour wait before his next train could travel on south. He found himself in Shrieveport. A border town resting in the corner of Louisiana, Texas, Arkansas, and Indian Territory. Nothing in Shrieveport he wanted to see, so he opted to wait out the time in the train station. Nothing anywhere he really wanted to see or do but get back to Sweet Penchant. It was there that Maggie held the other two letters to make his life complete.

He picked up a newspaper from the wooden bench in a corner and read an article about New England granite. It was lauded as second to none other and had been used in building the Havemeyer mansion, the Union Trust Building, and the Carnegie Library. Everett had had occasion to be in all three of those buildings and yes, they were awe inspiring, but the thought of visiting any of them again didn't make his heart ache like the memories of Sweet Penchant did at that moment. He laid the paper aside and watched a train unload. People hugging people. Mothers with babies in arms snuggled up just briefly for a public kiss with beaming men. Grandmothers reluctant to let go of little ones once they were in their arms. Life went on before Everett's eyes while his own stood still. He picked up the paper again and looked through a multi-page article concerning the new construction in Boston. Houses so enormous they could swallow up Sweet Penchant in a mere fraction of the space. Yet, in all their black and white splendor, they didn't whisper his name and call him home to plant sugar in the rich black bottomland or to row a *pirogue* down the bayou to the island with Maggie.

Another article caught his eye and he didn't pay any attention to the next group deboarding. He read about a new train station underway in New York City. The reporter quoted a city official as saying it was one "of which the city may well be proud." Well, that was certainly good news. The old Union Depot needed cleaning up and replacing.

He laid the paper aside for a while and watched the people again. Such an interesting array of them. Poor, rich, skinny, fat. The train didn't care what they looked like as long as they could lay their money on the line. Folks began to claim their baggage and disappear in the midst of much smiling and talking; but Everett didn't smile. Not yet. Not until he'd laid his two letters on the line at Sweet Penchant. Which two letters did he hold? He wondered. L . . . O . . . V . . . E. Maggie held two and he had the others. Which ones were his and which were hers? Did it matter? If they weren't all together, it wasn't a word anyway.

A different newspaper left behind by some bored, restless passenger caught his eye. It was folded into a quarter section with a poem lying face up. He picked it up to look closer and a line jumped off the page and straight into his heart. *Through you I learn what life may be.* He looked up to see who the author was and found it was entitled "Purification" and had been written by George Edgar Montgomery. Everett hadn't read the man's works before, but determined he'd do a little research when he had time. He wondered briefly if Mr. Montgomery had possibly met Maggie somewhere in his lifetime?

Maggie awoke with a start when the train stopped. Surely she hadn't slept that long? The porter knocked on her door and identified himself. He was there to take her baggage out onto the dock while she waited for the next northbound train. She rubbed the sleep from her eyes and quickly stowed Everett's robe in the trunk before she opened the door.

Her stomach grumbled, reminding her she'd not eaten since the day before. She promised that if it didn't do something stupid and cause her to faint in a pile of faded calico that she would find a dining room and feed it promptly. She stepped into the huge rail station and followed her nose to the only available table in the whole place. She shuddered when she looked at the prices on the menu but ordered a ham sandwich and a fruit cup anyway.

Maggie loved watching the people. A young couple gazed into each other's eyes at one table and reminded her of the honeymooning couple in the first train she and Everett had been on. An older lady said something hateful to the man across the table from her and he responded in like manner. Both of them set their jaws in a firm line of anger. *Don't be mad,* Maggie tried to reach them through her thoughts. *It's such a waste of precious time. You have each other and have had for many years, I'd be willing to bet. Don't waste a single minute on fighting when you could be loving, even at your age . . .*

The waiter brought her sandwich and fruit cup and she forgot about people while she devoured the food. Another train unloaded and people waited at the edge of the dining room for those who were eating to finish so they could take their tables. Maggie reluctantly gave up her table and meandered toward the waiting room. She'd find a corner and wait there.

Everett shuffled the two papers into a neat pile and laid them on the far end of the bench. A prickly sensation made his heart flutter; not totally unlike the way it reacted when he kissed Maggie those few times. She must be thinking about him. That brought a smile to his face.

Maggie sat down on the end of the bench. The man sitting at the other end, scarcely eight feet away, the one with his back to her as he folded his newspapers into a neat pile, reminded her of Everett. Dark hair. Wearing a dark overcoat. The hair on her arms stood up and her heart skipped a beat, but she reminded herself that Everett was back in Dodsworth by now. All he had had to do was file the papers and then he was going home.

Besides, all a man had to have was a head full of black hair and he reminded her of Everett. Even the porter had reminded her of Everett when she opened the door to her sleeper earlier. He had dark hair and was the same height as Everett and for just a split second she just knew Everett was standing before her. When the porter smiled and looked down at her through clear blue eyes, she'd known she was wrong. And she would be again when the man on the end of the bench turned so she could see him clearly.

A baby cried on the platform and Everett impulsively turned to see what could be the problem. The toddler had fallen, but her mother had her in arms now and was comforting her. Someone had joined him on the bench. Someone with a gray coat. An ugly gray coat . . . one he'd never forget. Good grief! What was Maggie doing in the Shrieveport rail station?

"Hello, Everett." She stared him right in the eye without blinking.

"Maggie? What are you doing here?"

"I could ask the same question of you, Everett. You're

supposed to be back in Dodsworth by now," she said breathlessly, wanting to touch his overcoat, his arm, his face, even his fingertip to assure herself she wasn't dreaming. Her eyes could scarcely take in enough of him. Black hair combed back. Slight dark circles around his deep brown eyes. He hadn't been sleeping so well either.

"I'm going home, Maggie," he said. Home—where Maggie wasn't. She'd made up her mind where she wanted to spend the rest of her life, and it wasn't at Sweet Penchant after all. Little more than a week, and she was already bored with the solitude and the hard work.

"Home to Sweet Penchant?" she asked, amazed.

"Yes. Something you said made a lot of sense. My children, should I ever have any, need to be raised on the land. It's their inheritance. They can't love that which they don't know," he said, savoring every nuance of Maggie, even in that horrid coat. Her eyes looked tired, as if she hadn't slept really well in days. An errant strand of burgundy red hair had slipped away from the knot at the nape of her neck. He longed to push it behind her ear and kiss the soft part of her neck.

"I see," she said. So it was good that she was leaving after all. She'd simply go home to Dodsworth and tell them the truth. Everett couldn't abide her presence at Sweet Penchant on a daily basis, but by golly, before she did she fully well intended for him to know how she felt. It didn't really matter where she spoke it. Not if she walked up on the porch at their cabin in Dodsworth or if she just straightened up her back and told him what was in her heart and mind right there in the middle of the train station.

"Maggie . . ."

"Everett . . ."

They both began at the same time.

"You go first," Maggie said.

"I'd planned this in a far less public place," he said. "I'd thought about this conversation in the rose garden. You seem to like it there."

"It's peaceful. All of Sweet Penchant is peaceful. It's my favorite place in the whole world," she said.

"Then why are you leaving?" he asked.

"Because I can't stay there, Everett. I tried but it didn't work. I can't stay at Sweet Penchant. Not until I've said my piece. What I didn't say is coming back to haunt me every minute I'm there. Momma taught me to say my piece and I didn't do it. I was too scared of your reaction. Well, now I have to or I can't live with myself. I should have already done it, but I didn't. I let you go without saying what was in my heart. I stood right up and told you what I *didn't* like about you. Remember when we were standing in front of Preacher Elgin. I surely didn't stutter that day. Or any of the other days either. I didn't have a problem the day Carolina came to our home and was so mean. Or when she tried to get you to say you'd marry up with her even though she is engaged to Gatlin," Maggie said.

"Was engaged to Gatlin. I gave him my practice and she refused to go with him to Oklahoma." Everett's dimple deepened.

Maggie giggled, easing some of the tension in her shoulders. "I don't suppose she would. Sounds like old Gatlin got out of that bad deal by the skin of his teeth."

"Kind of like that," Everett said.

"Well, I guess I better 'fess up. I didn't like you at all. You couldn't dance and you were far too serious. But my crazy old heart didn't ask me 'bout my opinion in the mess we made for ourselves. And it went and fell in love with you, Everett. So there. Now I've said my piece."

"Oh, Maggie," he said, sliding across the bench until he was only a foot from her. "I was coming back to Sweet Penchant to speak *my* piece. I wasn't too shy or backward to be ugly to you either. I said mean, hateful things about you being unsuited to be my wife. Little did I know that you were the most qualified person in the world for the job. I'm only half a man without you, Maggie. Like you, my heart didn't get the message that I didn't want you to be a part of my life. I love you, my *cher.*"

Had Maggie heard right? Surely Everett hadn't just said the words she thought he had. "Would you say that again?" she whispered.

"I said I love you, Maggie. Would you be my wife and live in Louisiana with me at Sweet Penchant? I'll try to arrange a dance or two every year so you won't be bored." He waited. Perhaps she loved him, but there was a "but" involved. Like "but" we have to live in Dodsworth or Atlanta.

"How could I ever be bored with you?" she said in awe. He actually just proposed to her. He said he loved her and he was going back to Sweet Penchant. Maggie's dreams were coming true.

Maggie and Everett were suddenly in each other's arms, racing heart beats echoing in unison. He tipped her head back and looked deeply into those mesmerizing eyes and found a future that looked bright with hope and love. When his lips met hers, the whole world stood still. There were no people in the busy train station or anywhere else on the face of the world.

Everett changed Maggie's ticket from Guthrie, I.T., back to New Orleans, and told the porter to put her trunk in his sleeper room. Mr. and Mrs. Everett Jackson Dulanis were going home . . . at last. They boarded the train and Everett picked Maggie up, calico dress and ugly coat and all, and carried her across the threshold of the sleeper.

She used the arm around his neck to bring his mouth to hers for another hungry kiss before he set her down. "How long will it be before we can get remarried?" she asked.

"We don't need to do that unless you want to," Everett said. He threw open his rolltop steamer trunk. He brought out the divorce paper and handed it to her. "I couldn't do it, Maggie. I went to the courthouse every day and couldn't go inside. I walked the fields of Crooked Oaks until Eulalie and Jefferson thought I was crazy. I guess I was. With love for you. But I couldn't make myself go in there and file the papers. We aren't divorced."

"You mean it?" Her eyes twinkled with excitement.

"But if you want a real wedding with the big dress and all the people, we'll have one. It's only fair that you have one," he said.

"What I want is to be your wife, Everett. I could care less about all that big dress stuff. But I don't feel married to you, not really, since we was forced. I know I love you with my whole heart. It's just that . . ."

"It's just that we wouldn't have said those vows if your father hadn't been there with a six-gun on his hip and a blunderbuss aimed at my heart," he finished for her. "And those are binding for the law of the land, but not for the heart."

"That's it," Maggie said. "I just couldn't put it in words."

"Well, we are married. We aren't divorced. You don't want a wedding but you want to be married. So if you'll take off that ugly coat, we'll—"

"Ugly! My Momma and I worked for days putting this lining in this coat so I'd be warm all winter. How could you call something my Momma and I worked on ugly?" she flared up.

Everett threw back his head and roared. "My *'tite ange* . . . that means little angel in Cajun, darlin', which you'll be speaking before long, I'm thinking. Also, I think life with you will truly be a bed of roses, complete with thorns. The coat is ugly. I want you to throw it away."

"No, I won't throw it away. I'll keep it to remind me always of the day you said you loved me. Loved plain old Maggie for herself, even in an ugly coat," she said, removing the coat and hanging it on a hook on the back of the door.

"Now. I want to repeat my wedding vows, only this time I mean them with my whole heart." He took her hands in his and stared deeply into the soul of Maggie Listen Dulanis—the soul that was entangled with his own so well that the two were definitely one.

"I, Everett Jackson Dulanis, take you, Maggie Laura Listen, to be my lawfully wedded wife. To have and to hold, through sickness and health, through poverty and wealth. I promise to share everything that I am or ever will be with you, to keep you near me forever," he said seriously.

"I, Maggie Laura Listen, take you, Everett Jackson Dulanis, to be my lawfully wedded husband. I do this of my own free accord because I love you with my whole heart. It's with that love that I truly come to you as a wife, and that love that will keep us through this life and the one to come. I love you, Everett," she said just as seriously.

She tore the divorce paper into a million tiny pieces, opened the train window, and threw them out, watching them fall on the earth in a wild array of confetti before she turned back around to face her husband.

"Let's celebrate with another kiss," she said.

"With pleasure." He tipped her chin back with his fist. The kiss held all the promise of a long and happy life together, where all the letters of the word love blended together perfectly.

There was unity . . . and finally, a real eternal union, surrounded by Maggie's love.